"I was yours before you ever touched me,"
Rylan said quietly.

Kirsten shut her eyes and turned away. "Please don't—"

"Why shouldn't I tell you? You already know it anyway. I've made no secret of it. I want you." He saw her swallow hard. "I heard you crying out and barely took the time to pull on my shorts before running to you. The moment I took you in my arms, touched you, kissed you, I was ready to make love to you."

He caressed her cheek with his fingertips. "Blame me for taking advantage of your emotional state after the nightmare. At first my intentions were honorable, but once I . . . Kirsten, I couldn't have kept my hands off you than I could have flown to China. . . ."

WHAT ARE *LOVESWEPT* ROMANCES?

They are stories of true romance and touching emotion. We believe those two very important ingredients are constants in our highly sensual and very believable stories in the *LOVESWEPT* line. Our goal is to give you, the reader, stories of consistently high quality that may sometimes make you laugh, sometimes make you cry, but are always fresh and creative and contain many delightful surprises within their pages.

Most romance fans read an enormous number of books. Those they truly love, they keep. Others may be traded with friends and soon forgotten. We hope that each *LOVESWEPT* romance will be a treasure—a "keeper." We will always try to publish

*LOVE STORIES YOU'LL NEVER FORGET
BY AUTHORS YOU'LL ALWAYS REMEMBER*

The Editors

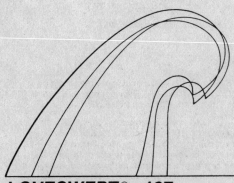

LOVESWEPT® • 197

Sandra Brown
Demon Rumm

 BANTAM BOOKS
TORONTO • NEW YORK • LONDON • SYDNEY • AUCKLAND

DEMON RUMM
A Bantam Book / June 1987

If you would be interested in receiving protective vinyl
covers for your Loveswept books, please write to this address
for information:

Loveswept
Bantam Books
P.O. Box 985
Hicksville, NY 11802

ISBN 0-553-21826-3

Published simultaneously in the United States and Canada

PRINTED IN THE UNITED STATES OF AMERICA

O   0 9 8 7 6 5 4 3 2 1

One

"I let myself in."

He hadn't known she wore eyeglasses until her head snapped up at the unexpected sound of his voice. She whipped them off and dropped them on the stack of manuscript pages lying on the Queen Anne desk in front of her. Her red pen, too, fell from her fingers onto the manuscript. One hand momentarily covered her left breast as though to still a pounding heart.

"You startled me, Mr. North."

"Sorry. Actually I'm perfectly harmless." Compared to the bright, pristine room, he figured he looked like something that had suckled at the tattooed breast of one of Hell's Angels. Her haughty expression told him he didn't belong here. Smiling covertly, he set his canvas duffel bag down near his feet and slid off his sunglasses. "I knocked on the front door, but no one answered."

"Maybe you should have tried the bell."

She was miffed all right, he thought. One hundred pounds . . . and that was a generous guess . . . of irritated female. Prickly broad, wasn't she? Were these first few moments going to set the tone for the next several weeks? Not if he had anything to do with it.

One of his knees unlocked, throwing his body slightly off center and into that thigh-melting, mouth-drying, heart-stopping stance that had beaten Farrah Fawcett's poster as the all-time best-seller.

"Should I try another entrance?" He curved his sullen mouth into the suggestive smile that was as famous as his arrogant stance. "Obviously my timing was off on this one."

She didn't return his smile. "Why bother? You're in."

"Right."

She stood up and walked around the desk. Not until she had taken a few steps across the terrazzo tile floor did he notice that she was barefoot. She caught him looking at her bare feet, but she didn't apologize for them or go through any of those flustered motions and babbling apologies that women usually do when caught in dishabille.

Her small face was set in an expression that strongly suggested, "If you don't like my bare feet, that's just too damn bad."

What she was better off not knowing was that he liked her bare feet. A lot. So far, he liked everything he saw, from the top of her glossy, dark hair to those ten, tempting toes. She was wearing white jeans, which fitted her a tad too well. In contrast, her white shirt was at least three sizes too large for her, somehow far sexier than a skin-hugging T-shirt would have been. The wide sleeves had been rolled back almost to her elbows, and the hem was brushing her thighs. It looked like a hand-me-down man's dress shirt. He wondered if it might have belonged to her late husband.

In any event, she was adorable.

"Did I catch you at work?" he asked.

"Yes, you did."

"On the book?"

"That's right."

"Forgive the interruption. I know how hard it is to pick up a thought once it's interrupted."

Impatiently, she pushed her fringe of bangs off her forehead. "My housekeeper went to the market, so I'll show you to your room. Where's your luggage?"

"That's it."

He nodded at the ugly duffel bag. One split seam had been haphazardly repaired with silver duct tape. Scuffed, scarred, and stained, it looked like the sole survivor of a baggage handlers' training convention.

"I left my Louis Vuitton at home," he drawled sardonically. "This is all I can carry on my bike."

"Your bike?"

"Uh-huh."

She gazed at him and his duffel bag with repugnance. He wanted to laugh, but didn't dare. Instead he let his attention wander to the glass wall that provided a panoramic view of the beach far below and, beyond it, the Pacific Ocean.

"You came by motorcycle from L.A.?" she asked. "You didn't fly?"

"Depends on how you define 'fly.' The California Highway Patrol might have called it flying." He grinned at her over his shoulder and slid his hands, palms out, into the holey, threadbare back pockets of his jeans. They had seen better days. Better years. "Terrific view."

"Thank you. The view was one of the reasons Charlie and I bought the house."

Pivoting on the heels of boots which no self-respecting cowboy, not even one down on his luck, would have been caught dead in, he faced her again. "Charlie? You didn't call him Demon?"

"Hardly."

"Why not?"

"He was my husband, not my idol."

His expressive hazel eyes, bridged by sleek black eyebrows whose arches were pointed at the apexes, focused on her. Most people thought that Rylan North's incisive stare was a trick of camera angles and expert lighting, possibly a device the actor used to convey his vast range of emotions. But it was a natural, unaffected characteristic—one eyebrow a fraction of an inch higher than the other; thick, short, black lashes; unmoving, brown-speckled hazel irises.

Rylan didn't deliberately subject her to that unsettling stare. He was only trying to gauge if there was a hidden meaning behind Mrs. Rumm's words. Perhaps there wasn't. But perhaps there was. He was there to find out. He watched her nervously wet her lips and decided that the odds were in favor of his intuition being right on target.

"If you'll get your bag," she said in a breathy voice, "I'll show you to your room."

"I like this room." He wasn't ready to be shuttled off into a back room like a disobedient child. He wanted to look at her some more.

"I'm working in here, Mr. North, and you're a distraction."

"Oh, really?"

He learned something then. She didn't like being teased. Her lips formed a pucker of disapproval. How far could he push before she lost the rigid control she imposed on herself? He was itching to know, but now wasn't the time to test it, not when he'd just arrived. "Okay, I'll leave you to your work while I soak up some scenery outside. Is that all right?"

"Fine."

"Good."

He raised one foot, pulled off his boot and sock, and dropped them onto the floor. Then he did the same with the other foot. He took hold of the hem of his black T-shirt and peeled it over his head, ignoring her gasp of outraged surprise.

His shirt joined the heap of foot apparel on the floor. "Go back to work. I'll see you later," he casually tossed over his bare shoulder as he slid open the panel of glass and stepped through it. He walked around the swimming pool toward the steps that led down the rocky cliff to the beach, wondering if she was watching. He would have bet his next Oscar nomination that she was.

He was tempted to turn around and find out, but didn't. He had an image to uphold, that of being an I-don't-give-a-damn bastard where women were concerned. And I-don't-give-a-damn bastards didn't react to women no matter how attractive they were. He'd almost broken that unwritten law last week when Kirsten Rumm entered her lawyer's office and they met for the first time.

The appointment had been arranged at his, Rylan's, request. He had known the moment Mrs. Rumm came in, shoulders back, chin high, carriage militant, that she considered the meeting an imposition. Only her eyes had indicated any vulnerability. They had been wary.

Her tailored, linen business suit had made him ashamed of his appearance. He had been up late the night before reading the movie script and jotting dialogue revisions in the margins. That morning he had overslept and hadn't taken the time to shave. He had dressed in the first clothes his hands had touched when he reached into the closet, a pair of slacks and a raw silk sport coat. Beneath the jacket, his partially unbuttoned shirt was wrinkled. Thank God the rumpled look was in.

He had been suffering a pounding headache from lack of sleep and had kept on his superdark sunglasses because his eyes were red-rimmed and bloodshot. Without the sunglasses he looked like the habitual user of a controlled substance on the morning after a binge.

She wasn't late; he and his agent had arrived early, the limo having made uncanny good time on the freeway. While waiting for her, the lawyer and his agent had fallen into boring conversation. He had assumed his characteristic slouch in one of the deep leather chairs and dozed until the fourth interested party arrived.

As it turned out, he had ended up being the interested party. Kirsten Rumm had carried into that austere, overly air-conditioned office the scent of flowers. Not the kind one could buy bottled in West German lead crystal atomizers from the chic boutiques on Rodeo Drive. The kind of flowers Mrs. Rumm reminded Rylan of were freshly picked straight out of a grandmother's garden after a soft rain.

If he had been wearing socks, the sight of her would have knocked them off.

He didn't notice the crunching sound of his agent's arthritic knees when he stood up for an introduction, nor did he pay any attention to her lawyer's effusive greeting. For him the only sound in the room was the delicious, rustling whisper of one silk-encased thigh moving against the other as she crossed the carpeted floor.

"Mrs. Kirsten Rumm, Rylan North," Mel, her lawyer said, introducing them.

It was public knowledge that Rylan North had the manners of a goat. The last thing he'd showed any respect for was the Pledge of Allegiance. He treated one and all with unpardonable rudeness. But upon being introduced to Kirsten Rumm, he rolled out of the chair to his feet and shook her hand just for the chance to touch her.

The bones in her hand were as fragile as they looked. He wanted to press both of her hands between his and assure her that everything would be all right. Why he immediately felt she needed that assurance, though, he couldn't have said.

"Mrs. Rumm."

"Mr. North."

Her voice was like the rest of her, small, soft, and sexy. Like a tangible thing, it touched his lips; he wanted to taste it. It touched his sex; he wanted to make love to it. He was semihard before he even sat back down.

She took the straight-back chair Mel held for her. When she crossed her legs, Rylan caught a fleeting glimpse of her slip, cream-colored silk trimmed in lace the color of cocoa. He was glad he had kept on his sunglasses so that he could stare, without anybody knowing, at the deliciously forbidden spot where one shapely knee was bent over the other. She had beautiful calves and slender ankles.

The top half of her suit was . . . wrap-around? Was that the fashion term? Anyway, it folded across her breasts. When she leaned forward slightly, the material gapped enough for him to see the bra that matched the slip, the curve of a breast, and lustrous skin that was tanned, but didn't have that baked, leathery look of so many women who worshiped the

Southern California sun. Her strand of pearls dipped into her bodice and lay in the shallow valley between her breasts. He became entranced by the rolling movement of those pearls across her tan line.

She looked as helpless as an ice cream cone in a steam bath, but she wasn't. "Why am I here?" she asked bluntly, coming straight to the point after only a few banal pleasantries had been exchanged.

"I asked to see you," Rylan replied.

She seemed reluctant to look at him, which was odd. He was accustomed to women staring at him with awestruck speechlessness. "I know that, but why, Mr. North?"

"I want to come live with you."

For several moments she only stared at him blankly. Finally she looked at her lawyer and demanded, "What is this all about, Mel?"

"Exactly what Mr. North said. He . . . uh, he wants to move into the house with you for a while."

His agent jumped in. "Rylan feels that it's essential for him to occupy the same rooms that Demon Rumm did. That he *absorb* Mr. Rumm's private life-style, experience it on a daily basis."

She looked everywhere but at Rylan. He was tempted to remove his sunglasses since she found looking at him so disconcerting.

"Essential to what?" she asked after a brief silence.

"My characterization of your late husband," he answered.

"The request might seem somewhat unorthodox," his agent began to explain, "but not if you understand how Rylan works."

"Exactly," Rylan broke in. "And no one can explain that to Mrs. Rumm better than I. Leave us alone for a minute."

He wasn't used to asking nicely. His agent took

the terse order in stride. Her lawyer seemed appalled, but allowed himself to be led outside after a nod from Kirsten. As the two men left, she recrossed her legs and assumed an unapproachable and uncompromising posture in her chair.

"I want to come stay in your house for a while," Rylan repeated.

He wielded a lot of power in Hollywood. All he had to do was suggest that he wanted something and dozens of people began hustling around to see that he got it. But Kirsten Rumm wasn't impressed with his lofty tone.

"I'm sorry, Mr. North. That's impossible."

"Why?"

"I'm trying to meet the deadline on my manuscript. My book and the movie adaptation are going to be released simultaneously."

"I'm aware of that."

"The publisher has extended my deadline twice already. I can't ask for a third extension."

"What has that got to do with my staying in your house?"

His hands were negligently draped over the padded arms of the leather chair. One foot, shod in Italian leather, was resting on the opposite knee. He was reclining on his spine in a pose that was so uniquely his he could have had it patented. Rylan wasn't the least bit worried that his plan would fall through. On the contrary, since she had challenged his request, he was even more determined to get what he wanted. Why was the widow so resistant to this harmless idea? Did she have something to hide?

"I can't turn my house over to you right now," she said. "It would be very inconvenient for me to pack my notes and manuscript and—"

"I'm not asking you to leave."

"Surely you're not suggesting that we stay there *together.*"

A trace of a smile hiked up one corner of his lips. "Yes. Live there together. Just as you and Rumm did."

He lowered his foot and crossed his ankles, stretching his legs far out in front of him. Lacing his fingers together, he placed his hands on his stomach, supremely nonchalant. No one but he knew that his heartbeat had accelerated. Nothing as exciting or as unusual as Kirsten Rumm had happened to him in a long time. Lord, he was sick of people who fawned over him.

"Don't look so shocked, Mrs. Rumm. We don't have to share a bed." He let a count of three go by before adding, "Unless your sex life with him is vital to my characterization."

At that point, Kirsten had surged to her feet and turned her back on him. She dallied with several of the marble fixtures on the lacquered surface of Mel's ebony desk. She flicked the cigarette lighter and discovered that it didn't work. She moved the ashtray and slapped the flat side of the letter opener against her palm. Finally, bracing her derriere—which Rylan would have loved to squeeze—against the edge of the desk, she faced him.

"I think this is just a publicity gimmick that you and your agent dreamed up, Mr. North. I don't like it and refuse to go along with it."

"Do I ever pull publicity gimmicks?"

She glanced down at the floor. "No."

"Well then?"

"Maybe your avoidance of them is a gimmick in itself."

Rylan had always been a student of human nature. Even as a child he had mimicked people's reactions to certain stimuli and analyzed the motivations behind them. Kirsten's objections to his idea didn't mesh. Her iris-blue eyes weren't ringing true with what she was saying. She was saying one thing, but thinking another. His request had been met not only with disfavor, but with fear. Why? What could she possibly be afraid of? Him?

"You didn't want me to play your husband in the movie, did you?"

"No."

Anyone else might have been hesitant to give him such a truthful answer. He respected and appreciated her honesty. "How come?"

"My husband was gregarious, outgoing, friendly, and generous with his time. He loved crowds, loved the fans that flocked around him, and would spend hours in one spot signing autographs to please them."

As she spoke, she aimlessly wandered around the room. Suddenly she turned to him. "You, on the other hand, shun your admiring public. You're secretive. I've never heard anyone describe you as friendly *or* gregarious *or* generous. In fact, quite the opposite is said about you. You're hostile and temperamental. You don't . . . don't . . . *smile* enough to portray my husband."

"Maybe he had more to smile about than I do." Rylan subjected her to a thorough once-over, partly out of a desire to rattle her, partly because he liked how she looked a helluva lot. "Maybe you were the reason Demon Rumm smiled all the time. That's what I want to find out."

Her eyes smoldered with resentment at his sexist insinuation. He didn't blame her. He'd had his share of it and knew how debasing it was to be treated like a wind-up toy that was expected to perform for the pleasure of the one who'd wound it up.

In a voice as brittle as an icicle, she asked, "Isn't it a little late for you to be worried about characterization? I thought the movie was almost finished."

"It is. Have you seen any of the rushes?"

"No."

"You've been invited by the director to watch them."

"I didn't want to see the film. I still don't."

Rylan was surprised. "Why?"

"I was married to an aerobatic stunt pilot. When I sent my husband off to work every day, he didn't go to a nice, safe office job. Writing down some of the events I would rather forget was harrowing enough. I don't care to see certain parts of my book—certain parts of his life—recreated on film."

There was much, much more he had wanted to ask her then, but he held the questions back for a later time and more suitable place. "Well, for your information, the producer and director are more than satisfied with my performance so far. They think I've captured Rumm's smile and pegged his public image to a *t.*"

"Congratulations. So why are you beginning to worry about characterization now?"

"His *public* image, Mrs. Rumm." He stood up and joined her at the windows overlooking San Diego Bay. "I watched interviews, read interviews, gathered as much information about your late husband as I possibly could. Yeah, I feel like I've nailed his public personality."

He made a quarter turn to look down at her. "But what was he like outside the limelight? In private. With the exception of a few of the stunts, those interior scenes are all we've got left to shoot. I don't feel like I have a handle on who the man behind the legendary smile was."

"You know that he was daring."

"Or dumb."

Rylan knew he'd gone too far when she confronted him. "It took a lot of nerve to do the flying he did. How dare you suggest—"

"Look, I think Rumm was long on guts, but a little short on gray matter to even attempt some of the stunts he did. That's not to say that I take anything away from him for daring to do them. Okay?" She didn't speak, but merely glared back at him with open animosity. Raking a hand through his hair in frustration over her failure to see his point, he tried again. "I need to get inside his head."

"His life is an open book. Literally. I'll send you a copy of my manuscript when I've finished it."

He shook his head. "Not good enough. I need to touch the things he touched every day. Listen to the music he liked. Eat the food he liked. Occupy the rooms he occupied."

"That's crazy! And unnecessary."

He slid one thumb into the belt loop of his slacks, which he was wearing beltless. "You didn't think so when the leading lady wanted the same thing."

He spoke the words with the triumph of a gambler slapping down the winning ace. He'd waited until it was necessary for him to play that ace, keeping it to himself that he knew she had granted the very favor he was asking to the actress who was portraying her in the movie. She had spent several days with Kirsten in the house in La Jolla.

"That was different," she said defensively.

"How?"

"That should be obvious."

"Our respective sexes?"

"For starters."

They were facing each other belligerently when a

discreet knock came from the other side of the heavy
double doors.

"Come in."

"Go away."

They had answered at the same time, though in
different ways. After giving him a dirty look, which
he found cute instead of threatening, Kirsten crossed
the carpeted floor and opened the door.

"Well, what have we decided?" Rylan's agent asked
heartily.

"I'd like to speak with Mel alone," she said coldly.

Rylan gave her a mocking bow before leaving the
room with his agent. They waited in the outer office
with the receptionist, a Barbie Doll look alike. They
came a dime a dozen in Hollywood. She squirmed in
her knit dress like a caterpillar trying to work its
way out of its cocoon and gave him tentative smiles.
He ignored her. She offered them coffee or drinks,
both of which his agent declined for him.

"How'd it go?" the agent asked under his breath.

Rylan shrugged, wondering if the receptionist had
any idea how ridiculous her posturing looked. She
either had a back ailment or was trying too hard to
impress him with the proportions of her chest.

His agent continued. "It was probably a good idea
for you to ask her yourself instead of getting her
lawyer to do it for you. You do have a winning way
with women." There was a trace of envy in his agent's
voice.

Rylan only snorted and closed his eyes. "Mrs.
Rumm is immune to heartthrobs. She lived with
one, remember?"

"He was hardly of your caliber."

"Thanks, but sex appeal is all a matter of taste."

"What will you do if she says no?"

Rylan tipped down the opaque sunglasses and peered at his agent over the top of them. "Nervous?"

"As hell," the other man admitted. "Don't even think of walking off this picture. I haven't settled that dispute with Stan Kubrick yet. For heaven's sake don't get me into another one."

"That's what you get paid for. An astronomical amount, if I might be so crass as to point that out."

"Crass, my ass. Forgive the rhyme. Crass is the only way you operate."

That was unarguable. Rylan North had been known to leave a picture if he didn't like the "tone" of the film, if he felt that his character's integrity was being compromised. That was a word often associated with him. Integrity. More than any actor of recent memory, he strived for purity of character. To him that meant making no compromises for the sake of the Motion Picture Association of America's rating or box office sales or anything else.

If it weren't for the fact that he possessed incredible talent that had only begun to be tapped, that every camera in Hollywood was in love with his face, and that he had a box office draw that equaled and often surpassed Stallone's and Eastwood's, no one in Hollywood would have touched him. He was considered by all to be a real pain. Yet he was everybody's first choice when "important" films came along.

"Before you start gnawing those bloody nubs that pass for fingernails," he told his agent, "let's see what Mrs. Rumm has to say."

He dozed. The agent chewed his fingernails.

Finally they were summoned back into the inner office.

*   *   *

She had said yes, and now he was here, floating in the Pacific Ocean behind her estate. After the grueling days spent on the set, two months without a single day off, the spontaneous swim felt wonderful.

His eyes stung slightly when he opened them to gaze up at a cloudless sky. Kirsten Rumm's eyes were a deeper blue than the sky, he thought sophomorically. They sparkled like jewels. But something dark lay behind them, shadowing that sparkle. He would find out what it was.

He was here to research the character of Charles "Demon" Rumm, but having met the man's widow, he was certain that she would be his most valuable source of information, the key to the dead man's soul.

Rylan was almost as interested in Mrs. Rumm as he was in her late husband, and he already considered Demon Rumm one of the most complex characters he'd ever portrayed. Why would any man have such an unrelenting death wish when, to all appearances, his life was so damned terrific? Before he left this house, Rylan was determined to know.

He rolled onto his stomach and, with long arcing strokes of his arms, swam back to shore. The sea water sluiced down his lean, naked body, emphasizing his sleek and supple form. Droplets clung to the dark body hair as though reluctant to fall free of it.

Rylan grudgingly pulled on his discarded jeans, which he'd left lying on the beach. If the far-from-merry widow had eyed his duffel bag as though it were a loathsome creature that had crawled up out of the ocean, he could imagine how she would look at him if he walked back into her office wet and unclothed. Such an exhibition would probably confirm as truth every sordid, sensationalized story she'd ever read about him.

Because he kept his private life just that, it was the topic of broad speculation that ran the gamut from drugs to religious cults to sadomasochism. Recently he had been photographed driving away from an alcohol abuse treatment center, where he'd gone to visit a friend. But the story that had accompanied the photograph declared that Rylan North had been in the expensive sanitarium for the last six weeks to dry out after having been evicted from a plush night spot after he became drunk and disorderly.

Another recent rumor had him dying of AIDS. It was a popular belief that he must be gay and that his well-publicized affairs with a lady governor, his last leading lady, and an Olympic gold medal figure skater were staged to protect his secret life as a homosexual. He was just too attractive not to be, it was said.

None of the gossip diluted his popularity with either men or women. Indeed, the reverse was true. The tabloid stories only whetted the public's appetite to know more. And it wasn't just the moviegoing public that was rabidly interested in him. The mavens of Beverly Hills kept his agent's mailbox stuffed with invitations. He rarely attended parties. When he did go to one, it was immediately catapulted into *the* social event of the year. Rylan viewed it all with a jaundiced eye and ignored every rumor, except those that were destructive to someone else.

Even the Hollywood barracudas respected his intelligence, his talent, and his refusal to corrupt either for the sake of a buck. He chose scripts carefully and discussed the director's interpretation of them before ever penning his name to the dotted line of a contract. Even then he didn't hesitate to break a contract if he thought the terms of it had already been breached by the director.

He was indifferent to what the public thought of Rylan North after they left the movie theater. While they were in that darkened arena, he wanted the ticket holders to be enthralled by the character he was playing, not by himself. What the hell difference could it possibly make to the audience if he were gay or bi or straight, or what he ate for breakfast, or whether he wore underwear or not? For their five-dollar ticket, he owed them nothing except a couple of hours of entertainment. His obligation to them ended at the theater's exit.

He considered his good looks an advantage to being offered the best roles. That was the only consideration he gave his handsome face and powerful, well-proportioned body. He didn't fear aging, the curse of most movie stars. Maturity would allow him to play roles that were denied to him now.

All that taken into account, he found it surprising that he cared so much what Kirsten Rumm thought about him. In this case, the way he looked could be a hindrance rather than an advantage. His famous face might be a barrier between them and—

Between them and what? he asked himself as he climbed the steps back up to the house. She certainly hadn't put out any signals that could have been interpreted as come-ons. She seemed interested only in getting rid of him as soon as possible.

Beyond that, he had to be very careful about whom he became involved with on any level, for the other person's sake more than for his own. Kirsten Rumm had suffered tremendously in the past few years. He would have to be a prize sonofabitch to drag her out of one well-publicized heartache into another.

But all his good intentions fled his mind when he crested the hill and saw her through the glass wall. She was sitting at her desk, bare feet tucked under her chair. Her head was angled to one side. She was chewing on the cap of her red pen and, as he watched, mouthed the words to the sentence she was painstakingly constructing.

Apparently she had forgotten her houseguest. That piqued him. He felt a perverse desire to get her attention off her work and onto him. So, wearing his arrogant smile, a deep suntan, and his damp jeans, he walked up to the part of the wall that slid away to form a door and knocked.

She jumped and whipped her head around. She had on her glasses again and looked damned attractive in them too. They had thin tortoiseshell frames, which were not quite as dark as her short hair. Few women could wear a pixie haircut, having only that fringe around forehead, ears, and nape to soften the severe look. But it was a sophisticated foil for Kirsten's youthful face.

He opened the door. "Got a towel?"

Irritation oozing from every pore, she got up and left the room, but was gone only a moment before she returned carrying a beach towel. "Thanks," he said as she passed it to him through the door. He used it to blot the salt water from his face, but didn't dry the rest of himself. "The water felt great."

"Not too cold?"

Was she looking at his nipples? They were erect, almost painfully so. "Uh, no. Just right."

"Oh."

"Will it distract you if I lie out here by the pool for a while?"

"Suit yourself."

She was still treating him with that condescending air, which would have irritated the hell out of him, had he not guessed that she was using that snootiness to hide something. Maybe an attraction to him that she didn't want to admit, even to herself?

He draped the towel around his neck and saw her gaze flicker over his chest and all the way down to the snap of his jeans. Between his navel and the waistband, his body hair was wet and curly. At her involuntary display of interest, he felt himself grow thick behind his damp fly.

"Why don't you come out with me?" he asked huskily.

The invitation startled her. She glanced up at him and said quickly, "No. I've got work to do."

"Gee, that's too bad." Pouting, he slurred his words.

Obviously irritated, she briskly slid the door closed. Few doors were closed to Rylan North. Even fewer were slammed in his face. But that's what he felt had happened and it made him madder than hell.

Turning abruptly, he reached for the snap and zipper of his ancient jeans and unfastened them. Before he reached the chaise, and in full view of her desk, he stripped off the jeans and kicked them away. Then he spread the beach towel over the chaise and lay down on his stomach.

He tried not to wince as he mashed his protesting manhood between his body and the unyielding fiberglass chaise. Looking as innocent as a baby settling down for a nap, he rested his cheek on his stacked hands and closed his eyes . . . but not before catching a glimpse of Kirsten's astonished face through the glass wall.

Two

He didn't realize he'd dozed off until he gradually woke up. And then he was reluctant to move. The ocean breeze whispered across his bare flesh. Like a woman's softest touch, it caressed the backs of his thighs, his buttocks. The sun felt wonderful, its rays penetrating his skin, heating his blood. Though heaven knew there were parts of him that didn't need to get any warmer. Ever since he'd met Kirsten Rumm, there had been a low fire smoldering in his belly and groin.

The lady didn't like him.

That was a bitter pill to swallow, a hard, cold fact. Or was it? Maybe she liked him okay, but wasn't receptive to him because she was still steeped in grief over the loss of her husband.

Either prospect was depressing.

He did several push-ups before levering himself off the chaise. The diving board was springy and helped him to execute a perfect dive into the pool. He swam its length, then climbed the chrome ladder out. He reached for the towel and wrapped it around his waist. Because of the outdoor glare, all he could see in the glass wall of the house as he approached it was his own reflection. When he slid open the door, he was surprised, pleasantly so, to see Kirsten bent over her desk.

"Still at work?"

"Uh-huh," she replied without looking up.

He stepped into the room and closed the door behind him. She still didn't even glance at him. He was annoyed, until he figured out the reason. Did she think he was naked? He smiled a smile that she fortunately didn't see.

"Do you enjoy writing?" he asked.

"Sometimes."

"Is it difficult for you to write about your life with Rumm?"

"Parts of it."

"Which parts?"

She threw her head back and looked at him.

"Well, *that* got your attention," he said with a sly smile. "Which parts?"

"Would you like to go to your room now?" Standing, Kirsten tossed down her red pen. It was getting quite a workout this afternoon, he thought. She brushed past him and headed toward the double doors to the hall. She stood there tapping her bare foot, the embodiment of impatience, waiting while he picked up his duffel bag, his boots and socks, and followed her.

"I left my jeans out on the terrace to dry," he said.

"Alice will wash and dry them for you when she gets back."

"The housekeeper?"

"Yes."

"Has she always been here? I mean when Rumm was alive?"

"Yes, why?"

"Because I want everything to be exactly as it was when the two of you lived here." As docile as a puppy, he padded along behind her. "Everything except the sleeping arrangements that is."

She stopped so suddenly that he almost bumped into her. "What do you mean by that?"

Surprised by her knee-jerk reaction, he studied her face for a moment. "I mean that we won't be sleeping together. Will we?"

His timing was one thing that made him such a good actor. He was touted for the masterful way he delivered dialogue. Now, between his sentence and the question that followed it, there was a strategic pause. Brief, but obvious enough to drive a Mack truck through.

He had intended to tease her again. But as he watched Kirsten brush back her feathery bangs, he found himself waiting for a serious answer. The fantasy of sleeping with her had been lurking in the back of his mind. Suddenly it had jumped out at him from behind its cover like the spring-triggered monster in a spook house. It was instantly there, unavoidable and vivid and full-blown.

He wanted this woman.

"Mr. North, some women might welcome that remark. I don't. I'm not at all flattered that you invited me to sleep with you."

One of his eyebrows arched into its characteristic point. "I didn't invite you to sleep with me. If I had, it wouldn't have been so subtle. I would have come right out and asked."

There was only the slightest breathless pause before she said, "Well, save yourself the trouble."

Turning, she continued to lead him through the sprawling house. Effectively put down, he followed, remarking on her house, saying how much he liked it.

"Thank you," she answered. "It was my first choice when Charlie and I started shopping for one. I think he wanted something more traditional, but I talked him into this one."

Rylan realized now why he liked the house so well. It wasn't cluttered with carpeting and drapes and furniture. The beauty of the house lay in its starkness, the white walls, the tall ceilings with their bare beams, the terrazzo tile floors. Furnishings and decorating had been kept to a minimum, but every piece was perfect for its setting. Nothing detracted from the spectacular scenery beyond the glass walls.

"Did you always get your way?" he asked.

She stepped aside to allow him to enter the guest bedroom before her. She didn't quite meet his eyes when she answered softly, "No. Not always."

"Was the house a concession for an argument you lost?"

Instead of answering she pointed to the mirrored closet doors. "There's a bureau in the closet. You can either unpack yourself or leave it for Alice to do. The bathroom's through there." She indicated the connecting door. At the built-in bookcase, she slid open a louvered panel to reveal a wet bar with a small refrigerator. "I think you'll find everything you need. If not, let Alice or me know."

"Why do I feel like I'm being left at camp for the summer? 'Got your toothbrush? Got your extra blanket? Good, then say goodbye to Mommy.'"

Kirsten ignored him. "Mel said you wanted to go through Charlie's photo albums. I left them out for you in his study. It's through the door at the end of this hall. If you'll excuse—"

"Why don't you like me?"

Dammit, he'd had enough. He could think of a lot of occupations for her mouth to be engaged in, and issuing instructions like a drill sergeant was at the bottom of the list. He didn't concentrate too hard on what he would put at the top of that list because he was still dressed only in a towel, but he crossed the room in three angry strides to stand directly in front of her.

His bluntness caught her off guard. She kept her eyes on a level with his chest when she said, "I like you fine."

"You sure have a funny way of showing it."

"I've been hospitable."

"Hospitality I can get at the Holiday Inn."

He had backed her up against the glass wall, which ran the width of the room and afforded a spectacular view of the ocean. His body almost went into shock when she eased herself from between him and the glass, by necessity brushing the front of her body against his. He learned two important things: she wasn't wearing a bra, and, in addition to being teased too hard, she didn't like feeling cornered.

"What do you want from me, Mr. North?"

If she knew what a loaded question that was, she wouldn't have asked it. He couldn't give her the obvious answer, so he latched onto the first thing that came to his mind. "I want you to call me by my name."

"I do."

"You call me Mr. North, not Rylan."

"Is that your real name?"

"No, but it'll do."

She turned away to gaze outside at the geraniums blooming profusely in whiskey casks that lined the border of the deck. "All right. And you can call me Kirsten."

"Thanks. Now, why don't you look at me?"

"*What?*"

"You heard me."

"I look at you."

"No, your eyes slide over me occasionally, but you haven't fully looked at me since I got here." He was thinking that if he could look at her, her mouth, her figure, her bare feet, and threaten to disgrace himself behind the towel, then she could sure as hell look at him. His desire fueled his impatience with her. "Why don't you look at me?" he repeated angrily.

"I'm not a groupie. A gawker."

"I don't expect you to be, Kirsten."

She did look at him then. At the sound of her name, she raised those serious blue eyes to his. He felt himself sinking into them.

"Celebrities don't awe me," she said. "I was married to one. He was human and so are you."

He was human, all right, he thought. His entire body was quivering with the desire to demonstrate basic human needs. He wanted to press her cool, white clothes against his sun-warmed skin, to cup her hips in his hands and draw her against that part of him that was tenting the towel despite his efforts to keep it relaxed.

"You resent my being here, don't you?"

"Yes," she responded bluntly.

"Then why did you let me come?"

"I was under pressure from Mel."

"Your attorney?" He laughed shortly. "I only met him once, but it's obvious that he's gaga over you. He would take a flying leap out his twenty-story office window if you asked him to."

"I listen to his advice and this is what he advised me to do."

"Under the threat that I might leave the picture?"

"You admit that that was a possibility?"

"I've done it before."

"Well, I didn't want to be responsible for it happening this time. I want the movie to be finished as soon as possible."

"I see. Your sacrifice was for the sake of the movie."

"Yes. I'll cooperate with you, because I want you to get what you came for and leave as soon as possible, but don't expect me to entertain you."

She was doing it again, assuming that superior tone that grated on him like a metal file. He'd have to break her of it, but how? She didn't like to be teased, and the honest and forthright approach hadn't worked. Shock maybe? He decided to let her talk without interruption, giving her some slack before he yanked the rope hard.

"As I see it," she concluded haughtily, "the only way we can make the best of this awkward situation is to keep our dealings with each other on a strictly professional level."

"That's the way you see it, huh?"

"Yes, I do."

"Hmm. Then I have a suggestion."

"Well?"

"Start wearing a bra."

"Wha—"

"Because I find it hard to think of you on a strictly professional level when I can see your nipples through your shirt."

He'd gone this far. He decided to go for broke. It would serve to show her that he didn't respond to bitchiness and at the same time gratify an impulse that had been tempting him all afternoon. He raised both hands and lightly raked the backs of his fingers over her breasts, over the prominent crests of them.

Her reaction was almost violent. She swatted his hands aside and spun away from him, then faced him with her arms as straight and rigid as flagpoles at her sides and her fists clenched. She was breathing harshly. "Don't ever do anything like that again."

"You didn't like it?"

"Obviously I didn't."

His gaze moved down to her chest. Her nipples were hard, making dark, pointed impressions against the soft cloth of her shirt. "Obviously," he said hoarsely.

She marched from the room, but her bare feet were soundless on the tile floor and robbed her royal exit of its impact. She made up for it by slamming the door behind her.

"How long has she been resting?"

"She was in her room with all the shutters drawn when I came home," the housekeeper, Alice, told Rylan.

"Maybe you ought to check on her."

The look she gave him was scolding. "I made her take two aspirin for her headache and—"

"She had a headache?"

"That's what she said. I put a cold compress on her forehead and told her to lie down until dinner." Alice wagged a carrot stick a few inches from his nose. "She's working too hard on that book, that's what's wrong with her."

Rylan was unsure that hard work was all that was wrong with his hostess. Hard work and a headache weren't solely responsible for driving her into the privacy of her bedroom. He was. What he'd done.

Where did he get off, touching her like that? he asked himself. He wasn't a fanny pincher. Lechery had always disgusted him. It made him embarrassed for the women who had to suffer it. He sympathized with them.

So what had made him touch Kirsten? Granted, he'd been sufficiently provoked on several levels, professionally, sexually, emotionally. Still, he shouldn't have done it.

She had every right to be spitting mad. Anger he could deal with. What he couldn't understand, and therefore what disturbed him the most, was the fear he'd seen on her face. Or had it been fear that caused her upper teeth to clamp down on her bottom lip? Dismay perhaps? Over what? His caress? Or her immediate physical reaction to it?

Damned if he knew. The elusive answer had haunted him while he showered and changed and spent an hour in the study looking through memorabilia on Demon Rumm.

Alice had found him there and, hoping to glean some information about Kirsten from her, he had followed her into the kitchen to chat while she prepared dinner. Rylan had taken an instant liking to the housekeeper. Like her employer, she hadn't fawned over him, but had fussed about the sandy jeans he'd left on the terrace. Her bossiness endeared her to him.

Where the Rumms were concerned, Alice proved to be loquacious, but discreet. She hadn't betrayed any confidences, if indeed there were any. Avidly curious about movies and moviemakers, she asked him about her favorite actress, whom he had co-starred with.

He set up his favorite story about that particular actress while Alice grated cheese into a bowl. "So she walks over to the bed, as we had blocked it. I've got my back turned to her, see? I take off my shirt."

"I remember that. It was a yummy love scene."

"Thanks. *Finally* it came out that way. But on that particular take, just as I got my shirt off, she let go this bloodcurdling scream. I thought, 'My God, has my back broken out with leprosy?' But it seems that the crew thought it would be hilarious to put a Gila monster under the covers and—"

"No!" Alice exclaimed.

"Yes. When she whipped the covers back, there it was in all its horny, ugly glory."

Alice was raptly attentive. "What did she do?"

"After that initial scream, nothing. She laughed and went along with the joke. But the next day she paid them all back."

"How?" Alice asked, giggling.

Rylan popped a ripe olive into his mouth, sucking on it as he talked. "She got up early and while everyone was still sleeping sent her kids—they were on the set with her—around to steal their shoes. By breakfast, she had a pile of Reeboks and Adidas and Kaepas, with all the shoelaces tied together. Ever try to sort out forty or so pair of sports shoes and stay on a tyrant director's rigid schedule?"

"Who would ever have thought she could be such a cutup? She seems so elegant." Alice glanced at something behind his shoulder and smiled. "Hi, there. Headache better?"

Rylan swiveled his head around to see Kirsten standing in the doorway. She avoided looking at him as she answered her housekeeper. "Yes, thank you."

He had difficulty catching his breath. The afternoon had culminated in a fabulous sunset. As Kirsten moved between him and the view of it, he could see her slender body silhouetted against the gauzy sundress she was wearing. The bodice crisscrossed in front over her breasts and tied behind her neck, leaving her back bare. It would have been impossible to wear a bra with that dress. Only his preoccupation with her fluid figure prevented him from laughing out loud. She had worn the dress in defiance. He wanted to congratulate her on her gumption, but the sight of her left him momentarily mute.

"Dinner's almost ready," Alice said, turning her back to them to reach for something in the refrigerator.

Rylan used that opportunity to say, "Nice dress, Kirsten."

"Thank you."

He could tell from the way she looked through him that she didn't approve of his dinner attire. The jeans he was wearing were clean, but in no better condition than the pair he'd arrived in. His white T-shirt had a blurred, laundry-faded image of the shark that Steven Spielberg had immortalized yawning from it. He had tied his bare feet into a sad pair of tennis shoes. Long ago, he'd begun dressing to please himself. He wasn't averse to wearing a tuxedo if the occasion called for it, but his "casual" bordered on "sloppy."

Kirsten glanced at him. "I'm going to have a drink on the terrace while Alice puts dinner on the table. Would you care to join me?"

He knew the invitation was issued purely out of politeness, but he accepted it. "Sure."

"This way."

She led him through the glass door to a lattice-covered part of the deck that provided a view of the swimming pool and the ocean. Built into a corner of it was a bar. "I'm having a white wine cooler."

"Soda and lime is fine."

He read her surprise in the quick look she gave him, but didn't comment on it. "Thanks," he said when she handed him his drink. "This is a beautiful place. Maybe I should invest in a home."

"I thought you had one in Malibu."

"If the tabloids are to be believed, I have one there, and a ranch in Arizona and . . . hell, I don't know, an igloo in Alaska maybe."

"You don't?"

"I've got a one-bedroom apartment just off Sunset Boulevard."

That disclosure stunned her. "Why?"

Shrugging, he dropped down onto the low wall where she was sitting. Only he straddled it, spreading his thighs wide and facing her. "That's all I need." He laughed at her expression of disbelief. "Don't tell me you believed all that garbage about leopard-skin rugs, mirrored ceilings, and statues of pre-Columbian fertility goddesses."

"I thought it was zebra skins and Egyptian sarcophagi filled with cocaine."

She had a wonderful laugh, he decided. The sound of it was pleasurable in itself, but he enjoyed it even more, knowing that whatever anguish he'd caused her earlier was dissipating.

"I promise you that I don't have the hide of any animal in my apartment," he said. She lowered her eyes to the rim of her wineglass, which she was tracing with her index finger. "And none of the other either."

"I didn't ask."

"Yes, you did." He spoke so softly, his words were almost lost on the breeze that carried with it the ceaseless, swishing sound of the ocean. "With your eyes. Where are your glasses, by the way?"

Their conversation had dropped to an intimate pitch. Kirsten inclined away from him, cleared her throat, and spoke unnaturally loudly. "I only need them when I work. Eyestrain."

He stared deeply into her eyes, as though searching for signs of fatigue or stress. She stared back, treating his eyes to the same penetrating attention.

After a long moment, she stood up. "Another drink?"

"Okay."

She fixed them each a refill, pouring more wine than citrus juice into hers this time, he noticed. He eased himself off the wall and wandered around the gazebo, touching the blossoms of the scarlet hibiscus. They bobbed in the wind like cardinals nodding their heads in approval of a pontiff's decree. He slid the tip of his finger into the throat of one. It was an innocent gesture, but he was immediately suffused with a rush of sexual heat. Erotic thoughts of Kirsten's body crowded his brain, pushing aside all others.

He turned suddenly, guiltily, and saw that she was watching his hand. Her gaze met his. The impact was physical, as though no distance separated them. Her cheeks were filled with color almost as vivid as that of the blooms. Rylan knew in that instant that her thoughts were running parallel to his.

However, he knew better than to press the advantage. Instead he asked, "What's in there?" and tilted his head toward an enclosure.

"A sauna."

"Sounds wonderful."

"Feel free to use it any time. It's never turned off."

They resumed their previous positions on the low wall. His knee accidentally bumped hers. She didn't move hers away. He left his where it was. He was finding it damned hard not to stare at her. He studied her over the rim of his glass as he sipped his soda.

"If you don't want me to read your mind, you'd better wear your glasses all the time," he remarked. "Your eyes are too expressive for your own good. And very, very blue."

"What am I thinking?" she challenged.

"About me. You're worried about what's fact and what's fiction."

"It's none of my business."

"I'm living in your house. That makes it your business. Are you wondering if I'm going to whip out drug paraphernalia after supper?" She ducked her head, a silent admission. "I don't do any drugs, Kirsten. Short of a few pot parties in high school and college, I never have."

She looked for telltale signs of duplicity in his eyes. "No?"

He shook his head. "Do you?"

"No!"

"Then we don't have a problem with that." He sipped his soda. "Nor am I an alcoholic who's trying to stay on the wagon."

"You're drinking plain soda."

"Because I took a sinus capsule this afternoon. I have a bitch of a nasal septum."

Despite his attempted humor, her expression remained serious. "There have been reports to the contrary. About the alcoholism."

"False reports."

"You've never denied them."

"Denying them would be tantamount to giving them credence. Besides, I have better things to do."

"Yes, I've read about those too," she said with a faint smile.

"My sordid romantic escapades? Do you want to know about my love life?"

"No."

"Does it matter?"

"No, as long as . . . as long as . . ."

"As long as I don't practice anything too deviate under your roof."

"I don't think you would do that."

"Thanks for the vote of confidence," he said sarcastically.

"Well, what do you expect people to believe?" she exclaimed. "You never grant interviews. If all these rumors are false, you could clear them up if you weren't so secretive."

"But those false rumors don't bother me. Apparently they do you."

"How can you stand for people to think bad things about you?"

"It goes with my job."

"Still—"

Before he realized he'd done it, he clasped her hand to stop her arguments and to emphasize what he was about to say. "Look, if I went on '20/20' and cleared up one set of rumors, by the next morning another set would have been started. It would be time-consuming and energy-draining to come along behind them like a poop-scooper and clean them up." She laughed at his analogy. Smiling, he added, "As long as the people I love are protected, I don't let what's written in the gossip columns bother me."

A shadow crossed her face, dimming her smile. "Uh-oh," he said. "I see you're still concerned about my love life. If you want to know my sexual preferences, why don't you just ask?"

She withdrew her hand from his and mentally, if

not physically, put space between them. "As I said, it's none of my business."

He drew a deep breath. "I have loved several men, Kirsten." Her gaze swung up to his. "Relatives. A very few cherished friends. But I've never had a man for a lover."

Somehow his hand was now curved around her elbow. He was stroking the inside of it with an idle thumb. He knew the caress contributed to the trance his lulling voice and steady gaze induced.

"If I were gay, would I have gotten so hard when I touched your breasts this afternoon?"

Her wineglass, slippery from condensation, slid from her grasp and shattered on the deck. At the same instant Alice called her name from the doorway.

The housekeeper was the first to respond to the accident, though for an instant the three of them were held spellbound in the charged atmosphere that immediately followed it. Alice rushed across the deck, avoiding the puddle of liquid that was spiked with ice cubes and shards of glass.

"Kirsten, I'm sorry," Alice cried. "I was only calling you to dinner. I didn't mean to startle you."

Kirsten seemed to have difficulty standing. It was as though her knees had forgotten how to do their job. Rylan encircled her waist with his hands and held her steady until she indicated with a slight twist of her body that his support was unnecessary . . . and unwanted.

"It was my fault, Alice," she said shakily. "The glass was wet and I just . . . let it slip through my hand. Dinner's ready?"

"Yes. On the table. You two go inside and I'll clean this up."

Rylan thought that eating in the dining room was like eating in a goldfish bowl. Three exterior walls of the room were glass. It was supported on a precipice that jutted over a steep rock cliff, which gave one a sense of being suspended in midair. The only furnishings were the dining chairs and a glass slab table resting on two brass rams' heads, their horns curling backward to form the legs of the table. Crystal candlesticks held burning white candles that filled the room with the scent of frangipani. In the center of the table a bud vase held three stalks of lilies of the valley. It was simple and elegant.

"Smart decorator," he said, holding Kirsten's chair.

"I did it."

"I like your taste."

After directing a hard glance at him over her shoulder, she seemed to reach the conclusion that his words carried no double meaning and stiffly sat down.

"Thank you."

She filled their plates with taco salad and their glasses with ice water. After folding her napkin in her lap and passing him a basket of crisp tortilla chips, she began eating. He watched her, knowing that her precise movements were an indication of tension.

"You seem upset. Are you?"

Her fork made a terrible racket as it clattered to her plate. "Yes, I'm upset!" she whispered fiercely, aware of Alice's mindless humming in the kitchen as she worked. "I don't want you to talk to me like that."

"Like what? You mean the reference I made to—"

She held up both hands. "Don't say it again. I haven't encouraged you to say . . . *think* . . . like that about me."

"No," he said quietly, laying his own fork on his plate, "you haven't."

"Then why did you do it?"

For ponderous moments, he toyed with his water glass while he stared at her. "I'm attracted to you, Kirsten."

She swallowed convulsively, though she didn't move another muscle. Even her eyes remained unblinking. Finally she said, "Don't pull this act with me. Don't practice scenes."

"I'm not."

He could tell that she initially thought he was trying to lure her. But the longer they stared at each other, the surer she became that he was being honest with her. Revealing little gestures—a flicker of uneasiness in her eyes, a darting tongue that moistened her lips—gave her away.

"This is business," she said.

He was heartened to hear an emotional gruffness in her voice. "Business is why I'm here, yes," he said. "But my attraction to you has nothing to do with business."

"You shouldn't be attracted to me."

"I didn't plan on being."

"Then don't be," she said miserably.

He reached for her hand. "I'm afraid it's not something I can turn off and on at will, Kirsten."

She pulled her hand free. "You'll have to. Or live with it in silence. In any event, it won't do you any good."

"You're saying no before I even make my pitch."

"That's right. I loved my husband."

He moved his virtually untouched plate aside and leaned forward, propping his forearms on the table. "Your husband's been dead for two years. I touched you today."

"Which you shouldn't have."

"Perhaps not. But I did." He moved even closer. "Believe me, Kirsten, you're alive. And even if your mind is closed to the thought of another love affair, your body isn't."

"I'm not going to have another love affair. Not with you. Not with anybody."

"You sound positive of that."

"I am."

"Why? Because you loved your husband?"

"Yes."

"All right. I'll buy that. Temporarily. But tell me, what made your relationship with your late husband so special that it ruined you for other men? What was it like being in love with Charles 'Demon' Rumm?"

Three

"Read my book."

"I have," he replied evenly. "At least the chapters that were made available to the screenwriter." He lowered his voice. "The book has been promoted as a 'tell-all.' I don't think you've told all. I think you're leaving out some very pertinent information about your relationship with your husband."

Kirsten removed her napkin from her lap and slapped it on the glass table. "Are you finished?"

"With this subject? No."

"With dinner."

"With dinner, yes," he said, and stood up.

She led him out of the dining room and into one of the spacious living areas. Alice had stacked and lit a fire in the fireplace behind a fan-shaped brass screen. This close to the beach, the evenings were cool enough to have a fire. It was a beautiful addition to the contemporary but cozy room. The shiny tile floor reflected the dancing orange flames.

But Kirsten seemed to regard the fire as a necessity more than an esthetic contribution. She moved as close to it as she could, as though seeking warmth. Curling into the corner of a plush sofa, drawing her feet up beneath her hips, and hugging one of the bright batik pillows to her breasts, she stared into the flickering firelight.

With no more respect for decorum than he ever showed, Rylan dropped onto the rug in front of the sofa. Lying on his side, he propped himself up on one elbow and stared at Kirsten until his gaze became as warm as the fire.

"Stop looking at me like that," she said crossly.

"Like what?"

"Like I'm about to start spouting ugly truths like a fountain with rusty water."

"*Are* there any ugly truths?"

"No."

"Then why do you get so touchy when we broach the subject?"

"When *you* broach the subject."

"I want to know what kind of relationship you had with your husband."

"It was wonderful. But, just for the record, I don't like your prying into my private life with Charlie."

He raised one knee and casually swung it back and forth. "I find it terribly interesting that you should say that. If you didn't want people to know about your private life with him, why did you decide to write the book? Isn't that a contradiction?"

Even the pillow she clutched to her chest like a shield seemed to expand with her heavy sigh. "Sometimes I wish I hadn't."

"Why did you, Kirsten? Money?"

She looked down at him scornfully. "Of course not."

"Glad to hear it. I wouldn't have approved. Why then?"

"I wanted to preserve Charlie's image."

Rylan sat up, Indian fashion, facing the sofa. "How do you perceive his image?"

"Like everyone else. All-American. Strong. Courageous. Moral. He was a good hero for the country's youth."

"You're referring to the antidrug rallies, the commercials against drinking and driving, and so forth?"

"Yes."

He knew she wasn't going to like his next question, but he had to ask it anyway. "Did he do one thing and preach another?"

Her eyes narrowed angrily. "No. He was an honest-to-goodness role model."

"Okay, I'm sorry. I just have this keen notion that you're protecting his sterling reputation."

"It doesn't need protecting."

"He had critics, don't forget. Many thought that he encouraged recklessness. He made stunt flying look so easy that he tempted unqualified, weekend pilots to give it a try."

Kirsten shook her head. "Every time he was interviewed, he stressed the danger involved. He was a nut for taking every conceivable safety precaution."

"But he glorified speed. That's right up the alley of a teenager whose parents are harping for him to slow down in the family Volvo."

"Speed and gravity were Charlie's challenges. His point was to let kids know that any obstacle, no matter how seemingly insurmountable, can be overcome if one works at it long and hard enough. He encouraged diligence and determination, the good old American work ethic. He didn't promote irresponsibility and recklessness. In light of some of the subculture heroes kids have, I think Charlie was a positive influence. I want him to be remembered for that and not for . . . for . . ."

"The accident."

The softly spoken word hung between them ominously.

Kirsten lowered her head until her chin almost touched her chest. "Yes."

Rylan scooted over to the wood box and added a log to the fire. Once the screen was back in place, he dusted off his hands and returned to sit near the sofa again. This time, he propped his back against it, placing his shoulder near Kirsten's knees.

"Other than continuing the legend of Demon . . ." he began, then added, "By the way, there was an argument on the set last week about which sports announcer actually dubbed him with that nickname."

Kirsten laughed. "Once he got so famous, many claimed to have. The fact is, no one really knows for certain. The story goes that someone said he flew his airplane like a demon out of hell."

"So some very clever person tacked your last name onto that and, voilà, a play on words." She nodded. "Okay, where was I? Oh, yeah, why did you write the book?"

"I've told you."

"You've told me why you did it for him. To preserve his heroism. Why did you do it for . . . or rather *to* . . . yourself?"

Rylan regretted having to put her through this. If he thought he could get to the heart of Demon Rumm's character through articles and photographs and film clips, he would have spared his widow this inquisition. But his intuition, which had been the bane of producers, writers, and directors for years, was telling him that Kirsten was the key to the man behind the all-American smile. If he had to probe her until her spirit was sore, he would. He'd gone to much greater lengths before to research a role.

When he had played a Depression-era bum, he had lived like one for weeks, riding the rails and living hand to mouth. When he had played a football player, he had worked out with the L.A. Rams, sparing himself none of the physical punishment a professional athlete puts himself through. When he played a Polish Jew in a Nazi concentration camp, he had had his head shaved and went without solid food for weeks.

He would take whatever measures were necessary to "walk in the shoes" of the character he was portraying on film. Now he was trying to get into Demon Rumm's skin through his widow. To all appearances, it was a very thick skin. It was going to be extremely uncomfortable for both of them.

"I had to lay it to rest," Kirsten said in response to his question. Rylan turned his head slightly to look up at her. She was gazing into the fire. "After the accident, there were so many details to take care of. The National Transportation Safety Board's investigation of the crash, the funeral." She shuddered. "It was such a circus. Press everywhere. Wailing fans clamoring to get close to the coffin."

She covered her face with her hands, dainty hands with a fragile tracery of veins and slender fingers with tapering, manicured nails. Her visible suffering affected him deeply. He ached to touch her and, with some small gesture, express his apology for this necessary lancing of her wounds.

But what could he do? Take her in his arms and hold her as he wanted to? No. She might read pity into that, and he knew she was too proud and independent to want anyone's pity. Holding her head between his hands and covering her incredibly sad face with kisses was also out of the question. He wouldn't be able to stop with light, comforting kisses. If he ever touched her lips with his, he would kiss her in the way that counted.

He settled for slipping his hand just beneath her skirt to cover her knee. He felt one tiny reflexive motion, a sudden contraction of muscle, but she allowed his hand to remain on her smooth leg.

She lowered her hands. Her eyelashes were wet, but she wasn't actually crying. "I felt separated from everything. Removed. I went through the motions, but I wasn't really there. Do you understand what I mean?"

For answer, he applied slight pressure to her knee. Her skin was as soft as satin. He had to will his fingers to remain still and not caress her.

"America grieved publicly, but I couldn't," she said. "I had always resented our high public profile, but never more than after Charlie died. I couldn't even mourn my husband's death without it being reported on the eleven o'clock news."

"Writing the book was a way for you to mourn privately, to bury him, to get it all out of your system."

She murmured an agreement. "When it's published, when the movie is released, I want to be done with it. I want to live a private life, to be just plain me. I'll never forget being Mrs. Charles Rumm. I don't want to. But I wish everyone else would."

The silence that followed was broken only by the snapping of the burning logs and, finally, by Alice's inquiry from the wide, arched doorway. "Kirsten? Would you like coffee served?"

Kirsten looked down at Rylan. He shook his head. "Thank you, but no," she told the housekeeper. "Go on to bed, Alice. I'll see you in the morning."

Alice said good night, then let herself out the front

door. Rylan had learned earlier that her apartment was separated from the house by a gravel, shrub-lined path. It wasn't until after she had left them that he wondered if Alice had noticed his hand resting on Kirsten's knee, partially covered by her skirt.

Perhaps Kirsten was wondering the same thing because she shifted her legs and sat up straighter. It was as though the demarcation lines on the playing field had become smudged and she had to draw them again, should there be any question of his stepping out of bounds.

"Are you sure you wouldn't like something?" she asked courteously to cover the awkward movement. "A drink? Dessert?"

"No thanks. What kind of date was Rumm?"

It took her a moment to assimilate his two unre-lated statements. "Date?"

"Was he polite, shy, amorous, aggressive, extrava-gant, a tightwad, what? Tell me about the night you met him."

"I'm sure you've already read that part of my book."

"I have. But I want more detail than you went into. What was the first thing he said to you?"

"No way."

"Please, Kirsten. I need—"

"I'm telling you! That's the first thing he said to me. 'No way.' "

"Ah, so *you* must have been the first to speak to him." Rylan propped his elbow on the edge of the couch, rested his cheek on his hand, and looked up at her with the grin that had beguiled half the popu-lation of the world. "Tell me about it."

She drew a deep breath. "I had just gotten my master's degree. I was feeling rather snooty, superior."

"Nothing's changed."

She glared at him, but he was relieved to see that

her mouth was twitching with the need to smile. "Most of the men I went out with were academicians. A girlfriend of mine invited me to go with her to a night spot. I knew it was frequented by servicemen and didn't want to go. But she had met this naval pilot, and he was going to be there that night, and she wanted to go, and I didn't have anything else to do, so . . ."

"You went," Rylan said, picking up the story. He extended both hands, palms out, thumbs together, and looked through the square they made as though framing the picture in his mind. "I can just see you. There you are, a pretty, petite lady who felt woefully out of place in a crowd of boozy, bawdy sailors and . . ."

". . . and after my friend deserted me to dance with this jet pilot, I was sitting alone at the table, trying not to look conspicuous. I noticed this guy across the room."

A smile broke across her face. A genuine, unguarded, natural, beautiful smile. Rylan's gut was wrenched by a spasm of jealousy for Charlie Rumm.

She continued. "He was tall, blond, good-looking, broad-shouldered, and he had a smile as arrogant as all get out. It said, 'Eat your hearts out, girls.' "

"And you hated that type," Rylan said intuitively.

"With a passion. But he wove his way through the crowd over to my table and sat down."

"How?"

"How?"

"How did he sit down? Did he slide into the chair? Drop into it? What?"

"Actually he turned it around and straddled the seat, then folded his arms across the back of it."

"Okay, thanks. Pardon the interruption. Go on."

"Well, he didn't say a word. He just sat there,

wearing this sappy grin and staring at me. I said, 'Stop staring at me.' And he said—"

" 'No way.' " They laughed together. "Then what happened? Did he buy you a drink?"

"He offered. I declined."

"How cruel."

Kirsten jumped as though she'd been shot. Her reflective smile was replaced by a look of astonishment. "That's almost exactly what Charlie said. He pressed both hands against his heart like Romeo and said, 'You wound me, fair damsel.' "

Rylan grinned. "Maybe I'm getting to know him better than I thought. Go on. What happened next?"

"His silliness made me laugh."

"That was the ice breaker."

"Yes, and during that weak moment, I agreed to let him buy me a glass of white wine."

"White wine, huh?" Rylan asked with amusement. "Were you wearing your glasses as you prissily sipped white wine amidst the hard Scotch and beer drinkers?"

Knowing that by now she was feeling more relaxed, he lay down on his back in front of the sofa, resting his head on his hands. Using his toes, he slipped off his shoes. His stomach was drastically scooped out to form a concave bowl beneath his rib cage, and he realized that he was hungry. Also slightly aroused. He wondered if Kirsten was aware of the bulge behind the fly of his jeans. Probably not. That had been his normal state since entering her house, that semifullness that hadn't reached the uncomfortable stage yet. If she had looked at him at all, she probably simply figured he was well endowed. The thought made him smile.

To justify that cocky smile, he asked, "What did you and Rumm find in common to talk about?"

"We talked mostly about him. Oh, he asked me polite questions, and was impressed when I told him I'd just gotten my master's degree in English. But he wanted to talk about airplanes and flying to the exclusion of almost everything else. He always did."

"Do I detect a trace of resentment?"

"Of course not!"

Her flare-up caused one of his eyebrows to *v* eloquently.

"I mean, flying was Charlie's life," she said defensively. "He'd been born to do it. For him not to fly was equivalent to not breathing. I understood that from the beginning, from that first night."

Demon Rumm had been a fanatic about flying and airplanes, Rylan thought. Men of his ilk were by nature required to be. But living with a zealot for anything wouldn't be easy or enjoyable. Wouldn't it tend to make the partner jealous of the fanaticism? Was that what Kirsten Rumm was trying so desperately to conceal, that she had been jealous of Rumm's obsession with aerobatics?

Rylan studied her for a moment, weighing the advisability of bringing up another touchy subject on the heels of that one. He decided that postponement would never make it easier to verify this point. "According to the script, Rumm told you that he regretted the end of the Vietnam war."

"He did," she confessed quietly. "He was a fighter pilot without a war to fight. I think he was actually frustrated when all our spats in the Persian Gulf were peaceably resolved. Not that he wanted to kill people. It was just that flying fast airplanes was what he felt destined to do. That's why he didn't extend his time in the Navy or become a commercial airline pilot as most of his friends did when their stints were up."

This was a facet of the man's character that Rylan wanted to explore further, but not just yet. "We're getting ahead of ourselves," he said. "Back to that night, did he come on to you?"

"Naturally."

"I'd have thought he was crazy if he hadn't. What was his line?"

"What do you think?"

She was challenging him. How well *did* he know his character? He squinted and tilted his head to one side. "Will you go to bed with me?"

She sucked in her breath quickly. "No."

"Is that what you're telling me or what you told him?"

The room grew very quiet, with only the logs in the fireplace crackling.

"You weren't asking for yourself," she said finally. "You were asking for him, weren't you?"

He grinned obliquely and was pleased to see that she was unnerved.

Without pursuing it, she rushed on. "He said I didn't look like the one-night-stand type and I assured him that I wasn't."

Rylan supplied the next line. " 'Good. Because I have something much more permanent in mind.' "

"You got that from the script."

He nodded. "He was a smooth operator. Seduction through the commitment angle."

"Maybe. Whatever it was, I fell for it."

"He swept you off your feet?"

"He made me feel giddy and breathless. After being around campus types who wore musty tweeds, affected Ivy League accents, and smoked pipes, Charlie was refreshing, with his rakish leather jacket, his Southwestern twang, and his dashing smile." Her blue eyes were glowing. Her lips were slightly parted and moist from frequent licking. Through them her breath rushed, lightly and thinly. "It was exciting just to be near him."

"I can imagine," he remarked wryly.

It was a new emotion for him, jealousy. He'd been struck. The fangs of the green-eyed monster had sunk in deep. Jealousy was pumping like poisonous venom through his system with each heartbeat.

He could imagine the effervescence she felt in her chest because it matched his own, that sexual awareness that made one tingle all over, that unspoken knowledge that something good was going on and that, given liberty, it would get even better. It wreaked havoc on one's erogenous zones and played Russian roulette with one's judgment. It was hell. And it was heaven. Poets and lyricists, try though they might, couldn't pen words to describe that twisting tightness in one's chest, that delicious pressure in one's loins, that fizzy fever in one's blood.

But, dammit, he wondered if Kirsten was feeling it vicariously through her recollections of another man, or was it for him? Was Demon Rumm responsible for that turbulence in her blue eyes? Or was Rylan North?

Apparently his eyes were as hot as his blood. His piercing stare must have frightened her. She moved quickly, swinging her feet to the floor.

"It's getting late and I've got five pages to rewrite tomorrow."

With one lithe movement, he was on his feet, facing her and bracketing her shoulders between his hands. "It's not that late. I'm not finished."

"Well, I am." She tried to squirm free, but he wouldn't let her go. He wasn't hurting her; his eyes exercised far more force than his hands. He could have compelled her to stay even without touching her.

"He asked you to dance, didn't he?"

"Yes."

"What did you dance to?"

"I don't remember."

"Like hell you don't. You remember everything else. What did you dance to?"

"What does it matter?"

"Precisely. What does it matter?"

Resigned, she said, "The crowd had mellowed out. They were playing a lot of slow dances on the juke-box. Neil Diamond, late Beatles, the Carpenters."

"Got any?"

He released her and walked over to the wall that had a sound system built into it. He began riffling through the wooden rack that held her compact discs.

"No, I don't have any of those," she said. "I don't think. I'm not sure."

"Then we'll improvise. Chicago or REO Speed-wagon? 'Careless Whisper' by Wham? What do you prefer?"

"This is crazy. Do you mean for us to dance?"

"That's the general idea. It's in the script. I need to research it." He chose the Chicago album and turned on the sophisticated machine. In a moment the music filled the room from various hidden speakers. He adjusted the volume to suit him and came back to her. "How did he hold you?"

"This isn't necessary, Rylan."

That was the first time she had used his name. It had been spoken in exasperation, but he'd take it any way he could get it. Smiling, he slid his right arm around her waist. "It's necessary for me."

"Why?" She resisted when he tried to draw her closer.

"Because we haven't filmed this scene yet. I want to get it right."

"I sound like a broken record. *Read my book.*"

"I have. It says in effect that you danced and that it was very romantic. Not much for an actor to go on."

"That's the director's job, to interpret the scene and put it on film."

"He'll set up the scene, Kirsten, but I'll bring it to life. By the time it's over, every man in the theater should want to be me and every woman you. Now concentrate."

The order was directed as much to himself as to her. Because with the contact of their bodies, he'd felt an onslaught of desire, and the only thing he could really concentrate on was being inside her. And he knew in that instant that it would happen. If he died trying, he would have carnal knowledge of this intriguing woman.

"I'm Rumm and I've just met an incredibly attractive woman that I've got the immediate hots for. What do I do? How do I act under those circumstances?" He yanked her up hard against him. "How did Rumm hold you when you danced? Did he hold you like this?"

He was holding her in the traditional waltz position, except much closer than most ballroom teachers would have thought appropriate or even feasible for intricate steps.

"Yes, at first."

Rylan began to lead, moving them in time to the moody strains of "Inspiration." Their dancing consisted of little more than swaying in rhythm, a brushing of two bodies electrically charged, a flirtation of masculinity with femininity. Vertical foreplay.

"Was he shy with you? Did he hold you this close?"

"Yes."

"To the first or second question?"

"The second. Charlie was never shy."

"Did he rest his cheek against your hair?" When she nodded, Rylan pressed his jaw against her temple. "Like this?"

"Yes, only . . ."

"Only?"

"Only he was a few inches taller. He had to bend down more."

"Well, I'm not going to dance on tippy toes, so we'll have to make do with this. Besides," he whispered, "I like the way we fit."

Their bodies did fit phenomenally well. They meshed perfectly. As though they had been blue-printed to fit together, his maleness nestled in her feminine softness. He couldn't stop himself from nudging her lightly. The cloth of her dress was sheer and giving, so that it was like there was nothing between them except his jeans. He could barely hear the music over the pounding racket his pulse made in his head.

"Anything else I should know?" he asked. He lightly blew against the wispy strands of hair that lay on her neck.

"He was brawnier than you. I remember feeling very safe when he put his arms—"

She broke off, and Rylan angled his head back and looked down at her. "Where?"

"Around my waist," she replied hoarsely.

He linked his hands at the small of her back and pulled her even closer against him. Higher. His body settled more deeply into the cove of her thighs. "Like this?"

She nodded. Leaning back slightly, she gazed up at him, as though trying to clearly distinguish Charlie Rumm's face from his. "His hair was lighter than yours. And curlier. The texture was different."

"Texture?" Rylan asked, pouncing on the word. "Did you touch his hair that night?"

She shook her head. Her eyes were filled with contradiction and bemusement. "I . . . you're confusing me. I don't remember." Her head fell forward onto his chest. Her arms were dangling loosely at her sides.

"Were your arms like this when you danced with Charlie, Kirsten?" She rolled her forehead against his sternum in a negative motion. "Where were they?" he asked gently.

Somnambulantly she raised her arms and looped them around his neck. She had small breasts. Her position only served to make the nipples more prominent.

Rylan drew in a hissing breath. "Is this when you touched his hair?"

"I think so. I must have run my fingers through it."

She matched action to words and it was all Rylan could do to keep from moaning as her fingers sifted through the hair at his collar. "How does mine compare?" He didn't give a damn. He only wanted to know how his felt to her.

"Yours is sleeker. Softer. Longer. Not as coarse. Not as curly."

He nibbled at the outer point of her eyebrow. His hands splayed wide on her bare back. "Were you wearing a backless dress that night?"

"No. It was fall. I had on a sweater."

She had the smoothest, most unblemished skin he'd ever felt. "Were you wearing a bra?"

"Yes."

"Then I am blessed." Groaning, he rubbed his chest against her breasts. When the tips tightened into harder points, he cursed beneath his breath. "Did you know he was getting aroused?" He rubbed his lower body against hers.

"Yes," she whispered.

"How long did you dance, Kirsten? Hours, I hope?" Though heaven knew that if they had, Rumm had more stamina than he.

"No, just a few songs. My friend came up and told me that she was going home with her pilot." She dropped her arms from around Rylan's neck and pushed herself out of his embrace. Short of reverting to caveman tactics, he had no choice but to release her. She walked over to the stereo, and when she switched off the music, it created a noisy silence. "Gallantly, Charlie offered to take me home."

"Gallantry wasn't his only motivation," Rylan muttered thickly.

She faced him angrily. "He was a perfect gentleman. He didn't try anything."

"I'm sure he was a gentleman." He took enough steps to reduce the distance between them considerably. "But I'm also just as sure that he was horny as hell and wanted more than anything to take you to bed."

"How would you—"

She never vocalized the rest of her question. He saw her eyes sweep down his body, saw her startled expression when they confirmed her suspicion.

"Right, Kirsten, you're better off not asking," he said softly. "Did Charlie kiss you good night?"

"Is it in the movie script?"

"There's an obligatory kiss in the script. But we want to sell tickets. Did Rumm actually kiss you that night?"

With an affirmative bob of her head, she began backing away from him.

"What kind of kiss was it?"

"You're the expert screen kisser. I'm sure that however you handle that first kiss will satisfy your audience."

"I'm sure it will too," he said with conceit. "This is for my own satisfaction. Was Rumm hesitant, not wanting to offend you? Or did he want that kiss so badly that he didn't give a damn if he offended you or not?"

His better judgment warned him that he was courting disaster. Neither of them was emotionally stable enough at that moment to handle what was about to happen, but he couldn't stop himself. He was either going to kiss her or he was going to die.

He had a lot to live for.

"Was his kiss sweet, chaste, and nice? Or was it hard, hungry, and carnal? Was it anything like this?"

He hooked his hand around the back of her neck. Before she could recover from her surprise, they were mouth to mouth.

All similarity stopped there if her first kiss from Charles Rumm had been awkward and bumbling in any way. If the young Navy pilot had bumped noses with her, apologized self-consciously, and tentatively tried again to do better, then their first kiss didn't even resemble the one Rylan impressed on her mouth now.

Instinctively he angled his head in the opposite direction of hers and sealed their lips together with just the right amount of possessiveness and pressure. If Charlie had given her several closemouthed, tight-lipped, dry kisses before working up enough courage to use his tongue, then Kirsten was no doubt surprised with Rylan's indelicacy. His tongue arrowed into her mouth with one swift thrust. It stroked her evocatively, unapologetically, masterfully.

Rylan knew that for as long as he lived he would never forget this first taste of her mouth. Lord, she was sweet. Her mouth opened up to his like a flower, then her lips closed petal soft around his intrusive tongue, hugging it.

He delved deeper, fearing that he might be going too far, but desperate for more, more. She responded. Her hands clutched at the waistband of his jeans, then her arms slid around his waist. Her body curved invitingly against his. He tilted his hips forward, until her thighs parted slightly and cuddled his hardness between them. Reacting strictly on impulse, he began lightly slamming into that marvelous softness with rhythmic movements.

Finally it penetrated his passion-fogged mind that her frantic movements weren't engendered by a desire to get closer, but to escape. He released her so suddenly they both swayed. For a moment they only stared at each other, lips moist and swollen from the power of the kiss, chests heaving, breaths rasping.

There were a thousand things he wanted to say to her. She gave him no chance. Spinning on her heel, she fled the room. He reached for her but clutched nothing but air.

"Kirsten!"

He chased after her, but knew it was hopeless. Even if he caught her, what would he say? That he was sorry? He wasn't. He would kiss her again, and just as passionately, if given the chance.

So, cursing himself, his impulsiveness, and the situation, he watched her retreat into the safety of the bedroom she had shared with her husband until the day he died in an airplane crash.

Four

Rylan had already been up for an hour when she made her first appearance in the study.

Nursing his third cup of coffee and a dull headache due to lack of sleep, he was reclining on one of the short sofas. Several pillows were piled beneath his head. He had been reading an article about Demon Rumm in a back issue of *People*. His feet, propped up on the arm of the sofa, were bare. So was his stomach between his sawed-off T-shirt and his denim cutoffs. He had dressed for comfort. But it wouldn't matter to Kirsten Rumm what he wore. She wouldn't like him anyway. Because she didn't like men.

That was the conclusion he had reached last night after hours of sleeplessness. Kirsten's reaction to his kiss hadn't been strictly aversion. Fear had been involved. Obviously she had some kind of deep-seated dislike for men and sex. Why else would she bristle like a porcupine every time one came near her? No wonder Rumm had had a long-standing death wish. The poor sucker had had an ice cube for a bedmate.

When he heard her enter the room, Rylan tipped the folded magazine toward his chest and, over the top of it, watched her hostile progress toward her desk. "Good morning."

"Good morning." She set down her cup of coffee and lowered herself into the chair.

Her unfriendliness miffed him. Frigid or not, a woman could be polite, couldn't she? "You're not a morning person, I guess."

"No."

"Good. Neither am I."

He rudely raised the magazine and began reading again, effectively cutting off any chance for conversation. A few minutes later, during which he hadn't retained a single word he'd read, he peeped at her around the edge of the magazine.

She was gazing out the window. Apparently she didn't know or care that he was alive. Her mind was a million miles away. Rylan took advantage of the opportunity to study her profile. Her features were neat, he decided, clean and pure. Her neck was long and graceful, a perfect pedestal for her small head.

She sniffed, idly scratched her cheek, then scribbled something in the margin of her manuscript. Her tongue darted out to moisten her lips. At that, he felt a spear of desire deep in his gut.

Dammit, he still wanted her.

She had every characteristic of a sensual woman. Why then the cold nature? Of course, there wasn't a frigid woman alive who couldn't be melted if handled by the right man.

Or maybe Kirsten wasn't frigid. Maybe her sex life with Rumm had been so fantastic that he was the only man she could see. Still. Either way, Rylan figured that he owed it to himself to find out.

He grinned slyly. He'd always loved a challenge and had never failed to rise to meet one.

Kirsten had become so immersed in her work that when he walked up to her desk a couple of hours later, she stared up at him vacantly through her glasses.

"What?" she asked after bringing him into focus. "Did you say something?"

"I asked if you were hungry."

She looked blankly at the tray he was carrying, then glanced over at the sofa he'd been lying on earlier. He answered her question before she asked it.

"I finished reading the article more than an hour ago and sneaked out. You never looked up."

She slid her glasses off and rubbed her eyes. "I got involved with this." She indicated the scattered sheets of manuscript.

"Interesting segment?"

Without waiting for her to grant permission, he set the tray on the edge of her desk and scooted it forward, displacing a thesaurus and a brass cylinder that held a collection of pens and pencils.

"Next to the last chapter," she answered absently, while mechanically moving things aside to facilitate his unloading of the tray. Suddenly, she snapped to attention, for the first time coming fully out of her writer's trance. "What is this?"

"Fruit. Blueberry muffins. Alice baked them from scratch. This is—"

"I know *what* it is, Rylan," she said, her voice laced with impatience. "What's it doing on my desk? Alice knows that I only snack when I'm working, if I eat at all."

"Yeah, she told me that." He hiked a hip onto her desk and plucked a handful of white grapes off their stem. "But as long as I've interrupted you, you might just as well eat."

Flopping back in her chair, she looked up at him with incredulity. Before she could recover, he asked, "Why did you live in the background?"

"In the background of what?"

"Rumm's life. I was particularly interested in that *People* article because it is one of the few that has anything about you in it."

"Charlie was the star, not I. He was the one everyone wanted to read about." She drew one foot up into the chair and wrapped her arms around her ankle. Her posture was sweet and submissive, but her attitude was defensive.

"Didn't he like sharing a spotlight? Even with his wife?"

"He wasn't like that." She viciously plucked several grapes, but she played with them instead of eating them. "There was no competitiveness between us. I didn't want to share his spotlight. But even with those who did, he was generous with publicity. Ask other stunt pilots. They'll tell you the same thing."

"So it was by choice that you stayed out of the public eye as much as possible?"

"Yes."

"Why? Were you jealous of the groupies who were always flocking around your husband?"

"Don't be absurd."

"Hmm." His expression was doubtful. "We filmed one scene in the movie where Rumm's career was just getting off the ground."

"No pun intended."

He saluted her cleverness. That she could tease him at all was a good sign. Maybe he was making progress.

"As I was saying," he continued, "after this particular air show, Miss Airhead—I can't remember her official title—trots up to him wearing a bikini and a banner—which was the wider of the two—and kisses him full on the mouth. She offers him unrestricted use of her body in the nearest motel room. Her dialogue goes something like, 'I'll show you acceleration and high-tech performance like you never dreamed of, Demon.' Fact or fiction?"

Kirsten dipped a spoon into a bowl of yogurt and fresh strawberries and stirred it, but didn't eat it. "It's a composite. Things like that happened all the time."

Rylan was watching her closely. "It didn't bother you?"

"This book and movie aren't about me, they're about Charlie."

"You're sidestepping the question, Kirsten."

"Which should be your first clue that I don't want to talk about it."

"So these incidents with other women *did* bother you."

She sprang out of her chair and clearly enunciated each word. "They were nuisances, Mr. North. Aggravations. Invasions of our privacy."

"Which I am now."

"Thank heaven! You finally got the message." She pushed back her bangs with a frustrated flick of her hand. "Stop badgering me about my personal life with my husband. It has nothing to do with Demon Rumm the aerobatic pilot." She rounded the desk. Rylan followed her across the room.

"You're wrong," he said. "A man lives with a woman. Whether he loves her, hates her, or is indifferent to her, she's bound to have some influence on his life."

He tracked her through the various hallways until

they stood outside her bedroom. She turned to confront him. "All right, granted. I would like to think that I had a very positive influence on Charlie's life. He did love me. He did need me. He even *liked* me, which is rare in most marriages these days."

She drew a deep breath. "But, I repeat, the book and the movie aren't about our courtship or marriage. They're about his career. If you want to talk about that aspect of his life, fine. If not, you're wasting your time and mine by being here, which I told you last week in Mel's office. Now, please excuse me."

She went into her bedroom and closed the door. Fifteen minutes later, having exchanged her slacks for a pair of shorts, she emerged only to find Rylan leaning against the wall waiting for her. He doggedly picked up the conversation exactly where they had left it.

"Did he talk to you about his work? About flying?"

"All the time."

"Did he ever tell you that he was afraid?"

His question brought her up short, but she hadn't taken umbrage as he expected she might. She had stopped to consider her answer carefully.

" 'Afraid' isn't the term I would use. Cautious. He was always extremely cautious. He calculated each trick aeronautically and mathematically before he ever got into an airplane to try it."

"What about superstition?"

She smiled. "Oh, yes, he was very superstitious."

At one of the terrace doors, she reached for the handle. "Don't you have something to do? Some place to be? When is your next call?"

"Not until next week. They're shooting scenes that I'm not in."

"Shouldn't you be studying lines?"

"I know my lines." She looked at him with aggravation. He smiled back. "Where are we going?" He followed her through the door she had slid open.

"*I'm* taking a walk on the beach."

"That sounds great."

"I usually go alone."

"Today you've got company."

Without giving her a chance to argue, he encircled her upper arm and helped her down the steep steps.

"I don't need your help," she said querulously. "I can negotiate these steps even on moonless nights."

"You come down to the beach at night?"

"Sometimes."

"While everyone else is asleep? Why aren't you?"

"What, asleep?" They had reached the beach. She withdrew her arm. "I have difficulty sleeping."

She didn't elaborate and Rylan didn't press her. He'd learned not to back her into a corner. Barefoot, they struck off down the beach, walking at the water's edge. The surf foamed around their ankles.

"Let me ask you a question for a change," she said suddenly, surprising him.

"Fair enough."

"Did you go into this kind of detail on the other segments of the movie? Segments not related to Charlie's personal life?"

"Naturally. I spent hours with the crew, chiefly Sam. That guy can put away more beer without falling down than anybody I've ever met."

Kirsten smiled at the mention of the flying veteran who had been Charlie's mechanic and friend from the day Charlie left the Navy and dubbed himself a modern barnstormer. Sam's failing eyesight had prohibited him from flying any longer; he had done it vicariously through Demon Rumm.

"I'm sure Sam had some wild stories to tell you," she said, laughing.

"Didn't he recount the same stories when you were researching your book?"

"The censored versions."

"You're probably right. His language is rather salty." He stopped and said seriously, "He holds you in the highest regard. He had nothing but praise for you."

He could tell she was pleased to hear that. It struck him then that she couldn't have been a detriment to Rumm's happiness or his best friend wouldn't have liked and respected her so much. That virtually ruled out the possibility of frigidity. Although, a man would find it hard to admit to another that his wife was frigid. So was she or wasn't she? Damn! It was still a muddle.

"The actor who's playing Sam, is he good?" she asked, snapping him out of his musings.

"Yeah, he's good. He's bawdy enough. But I don't think he's tapped into Sam's sentimental side."

"Sam's crotchety, but it's a cover-up for his heart, which is as soft as a madonna's."

"It didn't take me long to figure that out," Rylan said. Then he laughed, shaking his head. "The ol' sonofabitch sure ridiculed my flying capabilities though."

"Did you learn to fly for the picture?"

"I already knew how to fly. Sam just talked me through some of the easier stunt flying."

"So the rumor about you owning an airplane is true?"

"It's not a souped-up 707, if that's what you mean. Isn't it supposed to resemble a sultan's tent?" he asked with an ironic smile.

"Orgies at thirty-seven thousand feet."

He looked at her ruefully. "We can laugh about it now, but that story almost ruined the lady involved."

"The actress?"

"Yeah." He stopped, picked up a shell, and hurled it far out into the sparkling water. "We arrived in London at the same time to do that picture. What the press failed to point out was that we had arrived in separate airplanes. I'd met her only once, in the director's office with numerous other people present."

The wind tossed his hair playfully, but his mouth was grim and his eyes brooding. There was nothing cheerful in either his stance or his expression.

"When all that tripe hit the newsstands, it suggested that we were stoned when we got to Heathrow and in the throes of a scorching affair. Her current boyfriend wired her that they were through. Her mother telephoned across the Atlantic to call her a slut. She was so upset she couldn't work for days.

"That movie was her first starring role. The director was a bully. She was terrified of him and too damned lenient with her agent and publicist, who were both money-grabbing crooks." He drew a heavy breath.

"She was so damned innocent. Now I understand that her brain is fried. She needs pills just to get out of bed in the morning, and more to go to sleep. Cocaine has contributed to her paranoia. She's living up to everything the press prematurely wrote about her. The bastards."

He stood against the buffeting wind, unmindful of it. Without his even trying, the emotion his face conveyed was captivating. It was no wonder cameras treated it kindly, cosseted it, made love to it.

Suddenly realizing the moody reflections he had fallen into, Rylan turned his head and caught Kirsten staring at him. He gave her one of those sardonic smiles he was famous for. "Such is Hollywood."

He looked at her through speculative eyes, noting the way the wind was whipping her clothes around her slender body. Her blouse alternately billowed like a sail, then was plastered against her alluring form. "You're pretty enough," he said. "Ever thought about becoming a movie star?"

She laughed, but the wind snatched away the sound, leaving Rylan with only a delightful image of her smiling mouth. He ached to taste it again.

"Hardly. I don't have the talent or the drive or the discipline."

"No discipline? I wouldn't say that. You sat in that chair this morning, poring over the same page of manuscript for hours."

"That's different."

"How?"

"It's personal. Just between the words on that page and me."

"That's important to you, isn't it? Protecting your privacy?"

"Very."

His gaze moved over her. He studied her clinically, as a movie mogul might a starlet while he weighed her box office potential. "It's probably just as well you didn't try Hollywood. They might have messed you up."

He was hoping she would take the bait. She did. She asked him how she might be messed up.

"For instance," he said, "they would probably have wanted you to let your hair grow long. And it's so damn perfect for you this way." He cupped her head in his hands and followed the curvature of her skull and its cap of dark hair. He playfully yanked on the straight, wispy fringe in front of her ears.

Framing her face between his hands, he said, "Terrific eyes. Wide, intelligent, expressive. You certainly
wouldn't need glue-on eyelashes. Not with these."
He ran the tip of his finger over the dark, feathery
lashes.

"Good bone structure. High cheekbones." He took
her chin in one hand and with a swift motion, poked
his thumb between her lips and slid the pad of it
over her front teeth. "Straight teeth. Seductive smile.
And I know for a fact that you're a good kisser."

The caress was over and done with before Kirsten
could react to it. And while she was still docile with
astonishment, he moved his hands down to her
hips and sandwiched them between his palms. She
gazed at him in silent shock, but he didn't remove
his hands. It was now or never. He had to know.

"You're narrow enough through here." His thumbs
lazily rotated over her hipbones. The cloth of her
shorts, made like men's boxers, was so soft that it
might not have been there. He wanted to press his
open palm over the flat plane of her stomach and
slide his fingers down into the v of her thighs, but
decided that might be going too far. "You probably
wouldn't have to lose a single ounce." His voice was
so low, it was almost a growl.

She wasn't participating. If he had expected her to
collapse against him, tearing at his clothes, begging
him to take her then and there on the sand and
appease a primal urge, he knew he was in for a
grave disappointment.

But she wasn't resisting either. He drew small
encouragement from that. Was it stark fear or arousal
that had dilated her eyes and made her breath as
choppy as the whitecaps out on the ocean?

His hands glided up her rib cage and paused for a
heartbeat before sliding over her breasts. "They would

have wanted to pump these full of silicone." He pressed his hands over her, taking all of her within his palms. "And that would have been a damn shame. You're perfect as you are." His thumbs brushed the taut peaks. "Perfect."

She stepped back quickly. "Don't!"

Just as quickly, he reached for her again, because a split second before she stumbled away from him, he had felt her body's response to his touch. That shrinking, that tightening of flesh was her undeniable giveaway. He spanned her waist with his hands and drew her against him. "Don't what, Kirsten?"

"Don't touch me like that."

"Why not?"

"I don't like it. I didn't like it last night and I don't like it today."

His eyes bore down into hers. His were predatory, hers wary. "You're a liar. You like it a lot. That's what's bugging you."

"That's not true!"

She strained to get away from him, but his hold was unrelenting. "What aren't you telling in your book?"

"Nothing important."

"Uh-huh. How Rumm felt about you, how you felt about him, is vastly important."

With a sudden burst of strength, she shoved him away from her. "Leave me alone. For the last time, I will *not* discuss my private life with you or anybody. If you continue to pester me and subject me to your mauling, I'll have to ask you to leave."

As he watched her making fleet and surefooted progress up the steep steps, he expansively cursed his impatience and the erection that had precipitated it.

*   *   *

The road was endless. It was hot and dusty. In the rearview mirror of her car, she could see the cloud of dust she was leaving in her wake. It obscured everything behind her.

Her eyes scanned the horizon. She had to keep going forward. She had to get there before . . .

Before what?

She wasn't sure. But she had a terrifying compulsion to press on the accelerator and drive very fast toward—

Oh, God! That was it! She had to get to the column of smoke. She could see it now, as black and oily as a water snake rising up out of the desert. It was so far away. She'd never make it in time.

"Charlie, Charlie!"

She opened her mouth and tried to call his name, tried to tell him that she was coming, but the clouds of dust behind her were catching up. They filled her throat and mouth with heat and grit. She couldn't utter a sound beyond the grunting whimpers of a frightened animal who smells death. The swirling dust hampered her vision. She was able to see the black plume of smoke only occasionally now through the ocher cloud that was engulfing her.

Her sweating hands couldn't hold onto the steering wheel. It kept slipping from her grasp. Sweat trickled down between her breasts, too, and made her thighs slippery as they moved against each other in an effort to work the accelerator and brake, both of which were spongy and seemed to be sinking into the floorboard of the car. She could barely reach them with the tips of her toes.

But she mustn't stop. She must keep driving.

She had to get to the black smoke, which was like a foreboding inkblot against the painfully blue sky.

She finally reached the source of the smoke, a silver aircraft, as sleek as a bullet. Fire and smoke were belching from it at regular intervals.

She got out of the car. Charlie, no, no!

But wait! Thank God! He was sitting in the cockpit. Weak with relief, she laughed. It was all part of the stunt. The smoke. The fire. Was it all part of the crowd-pleasing performance? Yes, of course it was. Charlie always believed in giving the people their money's worth.

He looked at her and smiled. He winked and said something, but she couldn't hear him over the explosions that kept erupting from the burning aircraft. He should get out now. He might yet get hurt. She ran forward, but instead of getting closer, a deep chasm yawned between her and the burning stunt plane.

Charlie, still smiling, raised his hand to wave to her. No, no! One of his fingers burst into flame. Then another. Another. Until he wore a glove of flames. And . . .

She screamed in sheer terror.

HIS FACE WAS MELTING BENEATH HIS HELMET.

She watched the handsome features melt and run together until she couldn't distinguish them any longer. She tried to reach him, but her feet wouldn't move. They were stuck in the sand. "Get out, get out, Charlie, there's still time." But he didn't because the crowds—which had sprung up out of the desert—were wildly applauding his courage.

The flames consumed the cockpit until she couldn't see him anymore. She couldn't scream. Her own breath seared her lungs.

The hot sand scraped her knees when she collapsed into it. "No, no, no, no . . ."

Rylan wasn't asleep. When he heard the faint, muffled cries coming from across the hall, he was out of bed like a shot. He stepped into his discarded cutoffs but didn't even take the time to fasten them as he ran to her bedroom door and flung it open. The wedge of light allowed him to see his way clearly to the bed where Kirsten was thrashing in the throes of a nightmare.

He didn't stop to think about it. He didn't pause to consider his options. Calling for Alice never crossed his mind. There was no hesitation on his part as he dived across the bed and gathered Kirsten against him.

Her response was immediate. Her rigid body went limp. Her hands, which had been spasmodically clutching the sheets, reached around the back of his neck, where she groped for and held onto handfuls of his hair. He didn't mind. He hugged her tight.

"Shh, shh. I'm here. It's over."

She held on tighter, burrowing her face in the hollow of his shoulder. He wasn't certain that she was fully awake, though she had begun to cry. Her tears were warm and wet. They trickled down his skin. He hated them, loved them.

The nightmare must have been hideous to have produced the twisted expression of horror he'd seen on her face before she'd buried it in his shoulder. He wasn't going to dismiss the nightmare with platitudes about it being only a bad dream. Bad dreams were hell for the dreamer. For as long as she needed him, he would stay with her, until the demons were banished.

His hands were gentle. He smoothed them over her head, securing it beneath his chin. His palms skimmed her bare arms and shoulders, at all times keeping her pressed close to his chest. Shudders rippled through her. The dream might have ended, but the terror lingered. She snuggled against him.

Her sobs finally subsided, but she made no effort to move away. "Poor baby," he whispered against her ear. "You're drenched."

She didn't stop him when he raised the hem of her nightgown and used it to dab at her perspiring neck and chest. He tried to do it in a detached manner. But when he realized that the nightgown was all she had on, it was difficult to keep his touch impersonal. His unhurried ministrations elicited a soft purr from Kirsten. Finally, regretfully, he let the nightgown fall back into place, draping her hips.

He slipped his arm around her middle, and only then realized that her entire torso was damp with sweat, tangible evidence of her nightmare. Using both hands, he pressed the fabric of her loose nightgown against her body to act as a blotter for the moisture that had collected on her skin.

She felt so frail beneath his hands, no larger than a child. He thought he could probably span her rib cage with his hands. But when his fingers brushed the underside of her breast, he felt a womanly fullness that made him ache. He couldn't stop himself from exploring further.

He used his hands to support her breasts. He felt the sudden cessation of her breathing and prepared himself to be shoved away. Instead, to his immense pleasure and surprise, Kirsten clenched her hands tighter around his shoulders.

His heart was slamming into his ribs and into the body he held against him. He pressed the small, full mounds of her breasts, kneaded them. She didn't pull away, but actually leaned into his caress. He answered the hungry little sound she made with a groan of yearning. Her sweet lips moved against his neck, kissing it. The kisses grew more frantic.

"Kirsten," he whispered hoarsely.

God, this was good. So damn good. Kirsten wasn't trying to impress him with her stupefying physical dimensions. She wasn't a starlet trying to edge into his spotlight for publicity purposes. She wasn't bartering a screen test for sexual services rendered.

She needed him. Him, Rylan. Not him the movie star. This was honest. This was real. This was what all the man/woman stuff was about. And her quiet desperation was the biggest turn on he'd felt in years.

He was so hard, he had to bare his teeth against the pleasurable pain of it. What if his erection frightened her and she ended it now?

The sheets were damp and twisted around their legs. That made things awkward. He wanted to ease her back onto the pillows, to cover and protect her with his own body. Then, when she didn't feel threatened by him any longer, he wanted to kiss her mouth and stroke her finely made body until she was moist and open and as ready for him as he was for her.

But he didn't urge her to recline. Not yet. He didn't want to spoil it by rushing.

He ducked his head. Her eyes were still closed, but she responded by tilting her head up and back. Her lips were parted. He covered them with his own.

Her lips were cool, but her open mouth was hot. He kissed her lightly, several soft, pecking kisses, then rubbed his lips against hers. He licked salty tears from the corners of her mouth. Their tongues touched.

That ignited a powder keg of sensation. Heat suffused his chest and spilled down into his belly and
thighs. Immediately a strong, primitive arousal seized
him. Kirsten, too, must have felt it. She moved
against him restlessly. Her arms made hand-over-
hand climbing motions behind his neck.

He touched her nipples; she tore her mouth from
beneath his to utter a strangled cry. He stroked
them, tugged on them gently. More than he'd wanted
anything in his life, he wanted to take them in his
mouth, to caress them with his tongue for a very
long time, to feel them get flushed and hard against
his teeth.

But Kirsten became the aggressor. With an out-
pouring of passion he wouldn't have suspected her
capable of, she covered his throat with random kisses.
Then, inching her way down, she kissed his chest.
He cupped her head between his hands and followed
its aimless movements over his chest, loving the feel
of her breath soughing through his chest hair.

"You're beautiful, beautiful," she whispered.

She sank her teeth into the meaty muscle of his
chest and took a love bite. Moaning, he clasped her
head tighter. When her busily questing lips discovered his nipple in the whorl of crinkly hair, they
both froze for an instant. Rylan held his breath,
waiting, waiting in agonizing expectancy.

At first she gently closed her lips around the nub
of flesh, then daintily extended her tongue. His nipple beaded against the damp, flicking tip of it.

Incoherently, he called upon a deity. Murmuring
endearments, he sifted his fingers through her hair.
He tried to lift her head, but she resisted and moved
lower to kiss his stomach.

His cutoffs were still unsnapped and unzipped. He
knew that if she looked, she would see between the

open flaps of fabric a shadowy delta of dark hair. He dared not think what else might be visible. *Oh, no. Don't spoil it now. She would think—*

She slipped her hand into the opening and tentatively touched the springy thicket of hair.

"Kirsten!" he hissed.

Even through the red mist of a desire so potent it threatened to strangle him, he was amazed by her boldness. Granted, her touch was hesitant and inquisitive, almost bashful, but she *was* touching him. She had taken the initiative. He wanted to give himself over entirely to the pleasure of filling her hand with his flesh, but he was distracted by the sheer miracle of it happening.

Her caresses grew bolder and his body responded, until the merest glimmer of thought was extinguished and his attention was focused entirely on the milking motions of her hand.

"Kirsten, my God, Kirsten . . . beautiful Kirsten . . . not this way. . . . Let me . . ."

Suddenly she was no longer there.

Rylan opened his eyes.

Kirsten was sitting rigidly upright, holding her hands against her chest as though she had just snatched them out of the jaws of a man-eating beast. Her eyes were filled with horror and mortification. She looked at him as though he were the incarnation of the monster in her nightmare.

Softly saying her name, he reached for her. She shrank from his touch. She clapped her hands over her mouth to stifle a garbled scream. She continued to stare at him, her eyes glassy with fear and dismay.

Grimacing, he leaned forward, bracing himself on stiff arms. "I see. You didn't know it was me." The words were painful to say, almost as painful as the process of having to consciously squelch his desire. "Give me a minute," he rasped out.

In twice that amount of time, he slowly sat up and levered himself off the bed. On his way to the connecting bathroom, he zipped his shorts, but not without having to make some uncomfortable adjustments. He switched the light on in the bathroom, turned the cold water tap on full blast in the quaint pedestal sink, and dunked his head beneath it. He splashed his face and chest, but knew that it wouldn't arrest the fever that would rage through him for the remainder of the night.

He carried a wet washcloth back to the bed. Kirsten flinched when he sat down and extended it toward her. "You're soaking wet and it can't be comfortable. Bathe your face and neck."

Unintentionally he sounded brusque. He had tried to curb his irritation, but hadn't been very successful. He hadn't rushed across the hall with the purpose of making love to her. Her cries had drawn him. The only thing he'd had in mind when he barged into her bedroom was to be for her whatever she needed him to be. And that's what he'd done.

But now she was looking at him like he was Jack the Ripper. Hell, he hadn't done anything she hadn't begged him for. He'd hardly taken advantage. There wasn't a male animal from aardvark to zebra that could have gotten *those* signals crossed. She'd instigated the foreplay. He had responded. It had been her hands and her mouth that had started crawling all over him, not the other way around.

But when she buried her face in the cool, damp cloth and he had a view of the crown of her head, he wanted to lay his hand over it, to ruffle her tousled hair and tell her that everything was going to be all right. Where this feeling of compassion originated, he couldn't fathom. Given his present state of mind and body, it was ludicrous.

But it was there, a thousand times more potent than he'd first felt it that day in her lawyer's office. Kirsten might not be willing to admit it, but she needed him. Sexually. Emotionally. Every way.

When she was done with it, she passed him the cloth. "Thank you."

"You're welcome." He folded the washcloth and dropped it onto the nightstand. "You need a fresh nightgown. Where are they?"

"Third drawer," she said, pointing toward the bureau.

He found one in the dark and carried it back to the bed. After handing it to her, he turned his back and stayed that way until another quiet "Thank you" notified him that she had changed.

"Try to get some sleep."

Obediently, she lay down. He pulled the sheet over her, then bent down until his face was directly above hers. "What were you dreaming about, Kirsten?"

"Charlie."

All his facial features reflected a negative reaction to the answer he had expected. However, there was nothing but steely conviction in his voice when he said, "But I was the man you reached for."

Five

She liked men.

The theory of frigidity had thankfully been shot to hell last night. Sipping coffee as he watched Kirsten through the terrace door while she sunbathed on the deck, Rylan thought what a damned shame it would have been if that wonderful female body had been frigid.

But it wasn't. Not even close. Her mind might be frozen to the thought of making love, but her body damned sure wasn't.

Now the paramount question was, *who* was her body burning to make love to? He feared that he knew the answer and, aware of Alice working nearby at the kitchen sink, muttered a vile curse beneath his breath.

If he had met Kirsten when she was married to Charles Rumm, Rylan would have thought, "Damn that lucky bastard," but he would never have pursued her. He'd had more than his share of casual affairs, but never, *never,* no matter how strong the temptation or willing the lady, with a married woman.

He had lived with only two women, and each for a brief period of time. The first had been a struggling young actress, who arrived in the lions' den of Hollywood about the same time he had. They had found sympathy and security in each other's bed. After several professional setbacks, she had swapped her aspirations of serious acting for the easy bucks of porno flicks. Rylan had ended their relationship immediately. It wasn't so much the pornography that had turned him off, but her swift capitulation to failure and the ease with which she had sacrificed her goal. And then there had been their disagreement over the baby. Certainly that had entered into his decision.

His second live-in had been a real estate broker. Vibrant, energetic, ambitious. Her ambition had been one of her attractions until she had begun talking interest rates and percentages in bed. At that point he'd suggested an uncomfortable place for her to stick her For Sale sign. She hadn't taken kindly to the suggestion and had left their bed and their apartment in a huff, disparaging him for being jealous of and threatened by her success.

He held no grudge toward either woman, only felt extremely lucky that he'd escaped them when he had. So that brought him around to the question that he must ask himself: What did he want with Kirsten Rumm?

Was she to be just another casual affair, one in a series of such affairs that he always ended before either party, namely the woman, became too emotionally involved? Was Kirsten's resistance a turn on because it was so unusual for a woman to ignore him? Did it represent a challenge that he was damned and determined to overcome simply because the challenge was there?

In all honesty he could answer no to those three questions. His desire last night hadn't been rooted in his groin, but in his heart. He didn't just want this woman's body; he wanted this woman.

But she was going to be damned difficult to have if she continued to cling to a memory. He couldn't even begin to tear down their other obstacles—such as his stardom and her tenacious desire for privacy—until he convinced her that it was all right for her to love again.

He'd have to go slowly, be patient. It wasn't going to be easy. Ghosts had a way of assuming only the good traits of the deceased and none of the bad. How could a mere mortal possibly compete? Especially when his body was impatient. Every time he thought of Kirsten's mouth opening greedily beneath his, and how her breasts and their sweet crests responded to his touch, and how her hands had—

Crap! He couldn't start thinking about that again or he'd embarrass himself in front of Alice, who was asking him now if he wanted a second cup of coffee.

"No thanks," he said, setting his empty cup on the table. "I think I'll join Kirsten outside."

"Tell her that I'm going into the village for a while. I've got several errands to run."

"Okay."

He stepped through the terrace door. The sky was clear, the sun hot. Kirsten was lying on her back, unmoving, on a chaise longue, but he didn't think she was sleeping. She was wearing an electric blue bikini and sunglasses as large as saucers over her eyes.

"I wondered where you were," he lied. He'd been watching her for more than half an hour. He dropped down onto the chaise beside hers, sitting on the edge of it with his bare feet spaced wide apart, his clasped hands dangling between his opened knees. "Why aren't you at your typewriter?"

"I didn't feel like writing this morning."

"How come?" Behind the sunglasses, she was keeping her eyes closed. And he could tell by the way she shifted her position that his company wasn't welcome.

Too damn bad, Miss Kirsten. We're gonna talk about this whether you like it or not.

"The weather is nice today." Was Hollywood's leading man really uttering a line that banal?

"At this time of year in La Jolla, it usually is."

Feeling like a pervert but unable to stop himself, he watched the gentle rise and fall of her chest. Her breasts swelled into half-moons above the stretchy material of her bikini top. An application of suntan gel had made her skin glossy. Her stomach was concave, the hipbones slightly protruding because of her position. Her body tapered toward the triangular mound that lay in the cradle of her thighs. She had a faint birthmark on the inside of her upper thigh. He longed to kiss it.

After a lengthy silence, he thought, "Damn the torpedoes," and asked, "Are you upset about what happened last night?"

Kirsten sat up, swung her feet to the deck, and took off her sunglasses. Her face was as taut as the single word she said. "*Yes.*"

"Why?"

Her features were working with agitation. Rylan thought she might very well burst into tears. "Wouldn't you be if you were me?"

Standing, she yanked her oversized beach shirt off the back of the deck chair and pulled it on over her bikini. She struggled against the breeze and her own impatience to shove her arms into the uncooperative, flapping sleeves.

She entered the kitchen through the glass door; Rylan was only a few steps behind her. "We have to talk about it, Kirsten."

"Where is Alice?" He gave her the housekeeper's message. "Oh, yes," she said, massaging her forehead, "she mentioned that yesterday. I'm going to make one of those whipped orange drinks. Have you ever had one? They're delicious."

Prattling about nothing, she clumsily assembled the ingredients to make the drink in the blender. She almost dropped the pitcher of fresh orange juice when she took it from the refrigerator. Ice cubes were juggled from one hand to the other; she dropped most of them and they went skittering over the tile floor. The foil packet of dry mix which she took from the pantry refused to open. On the brink of tears, she cursed it before using her teeth to tear it apart.

She finally got all the ingredients into the blender's pitcher, but when she punched the button beneath the word "whip" nothing happened. She punched it repeatedly, making dry, sobbing sounds. "Damn. Damn! What's wrong with this thing?"

"It isn't plugged in."

His calm statement acted like a match to the short fuse of her temper. "You think you're so damn smart, don't you? So superior. Would you please just get the hell out of my house!"

Without interfering, he'd given her enough space to throw her temper tantrum. He'd allowed her room to paint herself into a corner with her own frustration. But it had gone far enough. He now stepped forward and gently held her by her shoulders. "Kirsten, you're not being rational."

"I'm rational!" she shouted, throwing off his hands. "Why won't you just leave me alone?"

"Because we've got to talk about what happened in your bed last night."

She drew herself up ramrod straight and said coldly, "Nothing happened."

Her refusal to acknowledge it sparked his own temper. Belligerently, he thrust his chin forward. "You had your face in my lap. I hardly call that nothing!"

All the color drained from her cheeks. Even her lips turned chalky. Her feet didn't move, but she swayed like a weighted inflatable toy that had been viciously socked. The groan that came from her throat was so soul-rending that it hurt him.

Immediately he threw his arms around her and held her close. He pressed his lips against the top of her head. "I'm sorry, Kirsten. I'm sorry. That was crude. Uncalled for. Forgive me for saying it."

She slumped against him, relying on his willingness to support her. "I can't talk about it, Rylan. Please, please just forget it."

"Don't ask me to forget it. I can't."

"You must."

"I can't," he repeated fervently. She gave him no further argument. Her head was bowed. He kissed her temple, wanting her mouth. "Are you embarrassed?"

Like a professional mourner, she rocked her head back and forth against his chest. "Embarrassed? Embarrassed? Of course I'm embarrassed." Abruptly she pushed herself away from him and flung her head back defiantly. In the same motion, she wiped tattletale tears from her eyes. "What did you expect me to be? When I woke up last night I was holding you, kissing you, caressing . . ." She faltered. "Caressing you like a lover."

"I remember."

His voice was as smooth and sensuous and unblemished as cream. They were both reminded of that single droplet of moisture that her fingers had discovered at the tip of his sex. That individual pearl of liquid that had dissolved against her tongue the instant he cried her name and she became aware of the bizarre circumstances.

She turned her back to him and lowered her head. He wanted to press a kiss on the nape of her neck, which was flushed yet vulnerable-looking beneath her shaggy hair.

"Please forget it, Rylan."

"I don't think I can. I don't think you can either."

She spun around angrily. "Don't flatter yourself. It wasn't you I was loving. It was Charlie."

Once, on the set of a Western movie, he'd been backlashed by barbed wire. Nothing had ever stung so badly. Until now. Her words affected him in the same way. He tried not to show it as he moved to one of the tall stools at the kitchen bar and sat down, hooking his heels behind the first rung.

"Finish making your drink," he said. He gave himself credit for his remarkable composure when actually he felt like driving his fist through one of the glass walls of Demon Rumm's house.

After Kirsten turned the blender off, she divided the thick, frosty drink into two tall soda glasses. She handed one to him.

"I'm going to take a show—"

He grabbed her wrist as she went sailing past him and pulled her to a halt. "Sit down. We're not through talking yet."

Her bottom landed solidly on the stool next to his, though he had exerted very little effort in getting her to sit down.

"We're through talking if what you want to talk about is last night," she said. "Just for clarification's sake, I took a sleeping pill before I went to bed. The doctor had prescribed them for me after Charlie died, but I'd never taken one. They look innocent enough, but are obviously stronger than I thought."

She exhaled a ragged sigh. "I had a terrible nightmare. You were only a—a presence. Something warm and strong. A bulwark. Given the circumstances, I can't be blamed for"—she paused to moisten her lips—"for what happened."

"If it's any comfort to you," he said quietly, "I did my part." Inquiringly, she lifted her gaze to his. "I was aroused before you ever touched me."

She squeezed her eyes shut. "Please don't."

"Why not tell you? You already know it anyway. I've made no secret of it. I want you." He saw her swallow hard. "I heard you crying out and barely took the time to put on a pair of shorts before running to you. The moment I took you in my arms, touched you, kissed you, I was ready to make love to you."

He leaned forward and said earnestly, "If we start slinging blame around—which in my opinion doesn't even apply because blame is indicative of wrongdoing—then I have to take most of it upon myself."

He caressed her cheek with the backs of his fingers. "Blame me for taking advantage of your highly emotional state after the nightmare. At first my intentions were honorable, but once I . . . Kirsten, I couldn't have kept my hands off you any more than I could have flown to China."

She pressed three fingers against her trembling lips. "I didn't mean to touch you. I was frightened.

You were there. You were real. Not the stuff of dreams. You were substantial. I responded to the contact with another human being, that's all."

"Not quite all, Kirsten. Not the way I remember it. Originally you were like a child seeking a place to hide, but before it was over, you were a woman wanting a man."

"And you exploited that, didn't you?"

He considered his answer for a moment. "I think it's fair to say that we used each other. Okay?"

She hesitated, but then said, "Okay."

"What was the nightmare about?" he asked after a brief silence.

His sudden shift in topics seemed to disconcert her. "Charlie," she blurted out.

"You've said as much. What about him?"

"I . . . It—it's a recurring nightmare. There are variations of it, but it always ends the same."

"How does it end?"

Her vivid blue eyes, made bluer by the reflection of the sky outside the windows, met his. "I watch him burn."

Rylan's heart plummeted and with it his hopes that he might be wooing her away from disturbing memories of her husband. He swore, softly, tersely, blasphemously. "How long have you had these nightmares? Since the crash?"

"No, before."

"Before?" His surprise showed. "You mean before it actually happened?"

"Long before." She slid off the stool and carried their glasses to the sink and rinsed them out. Neither of them had drunk any of the drink. "Sometimes I lived through them. He had a few close calls before the accident that . . . killed him." She moved to stand in front of the wall of glass that overlooked the valley below.

"Every time he went up," she said in a faraway voice, "even to practice, I wondered if he would come back. I would stand here for hours, staring at the horizon in the direction of the airfield, waiting to see the column of black smoke that would signal a crash." Her voice was weightless, drifting from her mouth as though she wasn't even conscious of speaking. "I was always vaguely surprised when it didn't happen and he actually came home in time for dinner."

"It must have been hell for you."

She nodded absently. "Remember asking me why I always stayed in the background? The reasons I gave you were valid, but the truth is that I didn't want anyone to see my fear. Every time Charlie performed, I was surrounded by expectant faces. People having a grand time, families on a weekend outing, the press corps excited about catching the stunt on film. No one seemed to realize or care that by entertaining them, my husband was risking his life. I resented his audiences for their disregard."

She roused herself and turned abruptly to face him. "You must think I'm a real nut case."

Rylan shook his head gravely. "No. But I think he was. Did he know how afraid you were?"

She returned to the stool and sat down beside him. "I suppose so. He should have. After we first got married, I would often cry and tell him that I was scared I'd lose him. I'd cling to him every time he left the house, begging him not to go up."

"But then you stopped crying and clinging."

"Not altogether, just not so frequently. And not in front of him. It didn't do any good. He was going to fly no matter how I felt about it."

At that moment Rylan hated the man he knew so well, but had never met. Had Demon Rumm materialized, he could have beat the hell out of him for all the years of anguish Kirsten had suffered. Rumm had been a selfish bastard.

"Why do you think he took so many chances with his life?" Rylan asked.

"It was his nature," she said carefully. "What makes a man want to climb Mount Everest or drive a race car? Not money. Charlie was a lot like you in that respect. He didn't really care about financial success or having material possessions. That wasn't what motivated him."

"The roar of approval from the crowds?"

"Maybe. He basked in celebrity. But that wasn't it entirely either. Taking risks was essential to him."

"To fill a deficiency?"

He knew instantly that he'd struck a nerve. "No," she said defensively. "He had everything a man could want. I didn't mean to imply that there was a deficiency. What kind of deficiency are you talking about?"

"That's what I want you to tell me."

"There wasn't one."

"So he just went out every day and flirted with death for the hell of it?" Rylan shook his head. "Uh-uh. I don't think so. I've studied motivation for years, Kirsten, and that doesn't jive."

"Some men are driven that way," she argued. "Danger is its own reward. Look at test pilots and animal trainers and . . . window washers, for heaven's sake. Taking risks is the nature of their business."

"Sure, but why do some men gravitate toward that kind of work? If you dug down into the psyche of each one, I think you'd find a common denominator."

"Probably a liking for their work. Just as Charlie liked, no, *loved*, his."

"More than he loved you?"

Her lips quavered, but she said staunchly, "He loved me."

"As much as he loved flying? Did you ever lay it on the line? Did you ever ask him to choose?"

"No, never! I never would have."

"Why not? Marriage is supposed to be a partnership, isn't it? Why couldn't you ask Rumm to give it up?"

"I *could* have. I didn't because I loved him too much to ask such a sacrifice from him."

"That's unrealistic bull."

"Have you ever been asked to choose between a woman you loved and acting?"

"I've never loved a woman that much."

"Which only makes my point."

Frustrated with her verbal adroitness, Rylan plowed both hands through his hair. She was holding something back. He could *feel* it. But he strongly sensed that it was prudent to back off once again.

"I'm not trying to badger you, Kirsten. I'm only trying to understand what motivated Rumm to risk losing his life, to risk losing *you*, day after day, and to understand what motivated you to keep silent about it. His stunt flying obviously terrified you. Did you know from the beginning what he planned to do when he got out of the Navy?"

"I knew he wanted to fly, but I thought it would be with an airline."

"And you didn't voice an opinion when he revealed his career plans?"

"Naturally I did."

"But he ignored your objections."

She sighed. "Don't put words in my mouth. I didn't object. It wasn't up to me to object."

"The hell it wasn't. You were his wife."

"But not his warden!"

"So when he said, 'By the way, Kirsten, I want to do hammerhead turns and barrel rolls at three hundred miles an hour,' you said, 'That's nice, dear. Is meatloaf all right for supper?' While shivering in your shoes and having nightmares, you just went along?"

Her eyes were stormy. "It wasn't like that. Charlie didn't start out breaking world records and trying stunts that had never been done before. It wasn't until later that it got so dangerous."

He came off his stool and loomed over her. "Later? Why later? What happened that precipitated him into taking greater risks?"

"Nothing." He stared down at her with patent disbelief. "*Nothing*," she repeated tetchily. "Just like any man who needs a challenge, he—"

"Kirsten, setting a new sales record and doing backward loops in high-speed aircraft aren't exactly comparable challenges. Dear Lord, no wonder you have nightmares." In a sudden move, he embraced her, drawing her off her stool and up against him. "And when you did have nightmares, did Rumm comfort you?"

"Yes."

To the marrow of his bones, Rylan knew she was lying. Her fingers were mindlessly flexing against the front of his shirt, as though grasping for something that had always eluded her. There was a giveaway unsteadiness in her voice, a trace of desperation that told him she herself wanted badly to believe what she was telling him.

"I think you wanted him to, but I don't think he did," Rylan said softly.

She started to protest, but no words came out of her mouth. For a long moment her eyes remained locked with his. Eventually her glance fell away. "You're right. Charlie dismissed my nightmares because he couldn't relate to my fear. He sympathized, but he treated the bad dreams like some childhood quirk that I would eventually outgrow."

Rylan drew her shivering body against his and rubbed his hands up and down her back. "So last night, when you reached for me, you thought it was Rumm. You *wanted* it to be him, finally giving you the comfort and understanding he'd previously withheld."

"I suppose so."

"Kirsten?"

"Hmm?"

"At what point did you realize it was me you were making love to and not Rumm?"

She looked up at him with a mix of pain and bewilderment. Then she flung off his embracing arms and fled the room.

"Don't let him drop you, Dylan, don't let him drop you."

Rylan, looking up into his victim's face, laughed. The child's brown-speckled, hazel eyes were much like his, and were rimmed with spiky black lashes. The child's hair, too, was dark, straight on the crown, but slightly wavy in the back and around his forehead, almost identical in color and texture to Rylan's.

Rylan was lying flat on his back on a chaise by the pool, his knees raised. With his arms held straight up, he was supporting a squirming, kicking little boy. Every few seconds, Rylan would make like he was going to drop the child and let the tension in his arms go slack. The boy would squeal, then convulse into wet, sputtering, slobbery giggles.

And every time Rylan's elbows would unlock a fraction, the child's mother, standing nearby, would gasp and say, "Oh, no! Oh, no, he's going to drop you!"

She was leggy and blonde. Dressed in a long peasant skirt and ankle-strap sandals, with her long hair swinging free each time she clapped her hands and playfully skipped around Rylan and her son, she looked extremely pretty in a free-spirited, sensual way.

"Pardner, you're gettin' too heavy and rambunctious to play this game," Rylan said, expelling a big gust of air and swinging the child down to the deck. He rolled to a sitting position and swatted the boy on the bottom.

That's when he saw Kirsten hovering just inside the terrace door. She had left the house hours ago, ostensibly to run errands. It had been three days since he'd confronted her about her nightmares and Rumm's indifference to them. She had avoided him ever since. During the day she stayed sequestered in her office while Rylan pored over journals and photo albums in Rumm's study. After virtually silent dinners, she retreated into her bedroom, leaving Rylan to entertain himself.

This morning, she'd been as chilly as the freshly squeezed orange juice Alice had foisted on them. Kirsten had drunk hers, then made a hasty escape in her Mercedes convertible.

Now, across the sunny terrace, their eyes met fleetingly before she disappeared into the shadows of the house.

"You've worn him out, Dylan. It's time to go," the blonde woman said, scooping up the child. She'd been unaware of Kirsten's clandestine appearance and withdrawal. Rylan wasn't sure why he hadn't waved Kirsten out and introduced them. There really wasn't any reason not to. But his avoidance of that had been for Kirsten's sake, not Cheryl's.

"Why do you have to go so soon?" he asked in a plaintive tone. "I don't get to see him often enough, Cheryl."

"I know. It's just that with my busy schedule and yours, it's almost impossible to get you two together."

Arguing was pointless. She was right, and he couldn't ask her to adjust her schedule around his. That wouldn't be fair.

He lifted the boy out of her arms. "Come on," he said, draping his free arm around her slender shoulders. "I'll carry him to the car for you."

A few minutes later he found Kirsten behind her desk, shuffling through the pages of her manuscript. She had changed out of the dress she had worn shopping and was now wearing all black: black slacks, black sleeveless pullover, black flats. He started to ask "Who died?" but caught the quip just in time. Under the circumstances that joke would have been in very poor taste. Besides, she looked great in black.

He passed up the opportunity to tease her about her somber attire and settled for a safe, hopefully peacemaking, "Hi."

"Hello," she said stiffly.

So much for peacemaking. "I wish you had come out. I wanted to introduce you to Cheryl and Dylan."

"I didn't want to intrude." She stacked several sheets together and thumped them on the desk with far more emphasis than was necessary to align them.

"You seem angry," he remarked. He was actually

glad that she was keeping her head down so she wouldn't see the amused grin he couldn't keep from breaking across his face.

"I'm not."

"Could have fooled me. You didn't even comment on my clothes, and I thought you'd be pleased to find me in something besides—"

"Rags." She gave his pleated designer slacks and sports shirt a negligent glance. "I'm sure you didn't dress up on my account."

"Say, you're not upset because I had guests, are you?"

"Of course not."

"That's a relief."

"That is, not as long as you . . ."

"As long as I . . . what?"

Looking as stern as a schoolmarm, she glared up at him through her glasses. "You know what I mean."

Enjoying her agitation, he propped one lean hip against the edge of her desk and folded his arms across his chest. "No, I don't. Tell me. As long as I what?"

"As long as you stay out of the bedrooms. This isn't a hot sheets hotel." She was busy moving objects on the desk from one spot to another with no apparent reason for the repositioning. "I don't want women running through here like there's a turnstile on the door."

"We didn't go into any of the bedrooms."

"Well . . . good. Then we don't have a problem."

"*I* don't. I think you might."

"As usual I don't know what you're talking about. What's more, I don't care. Will you excuse me, please, I haven't written a paragraph all day and—"

"What did you think of Cheryl?"

She clamped her teeth over her bottom lip as

though trying to get a grip on herself. "Cheryl? Is that her name?"

"Uh-huh."

She placed the stapler in a drawer, and slammed the drawer closed as though everything inside might try to escape. "From what I could see she's very pretty. Tall, blonde, and pretty." She spoke the three adjectives as though they were difficult words for her mouth to form.

"And Dylan? Cute little cuss, isn't he?"

"He looks just like you."

"You think so? Everybody who sees us together says that."

"How old is he?"

"Two. He's a dynamo. Cheryl can barely keep up with him."

"Maybe she could use some help."

"She's got help."

"I meant *yours*," she said with asperity.

"She doesn't need my help."

"Have you ever offered it?"

"Yes, and Cheryl flatly refused it."

"Don't you think you should have some input in Dylan's upbringing?"

"No way. That's strictly Cheryl's business."

"That's . . . that's idiocy," she sputtered.

He shrugged. "Cheryl didn't want any outside interference."

"And you settled for that?"

"I didn't have any choice. When she makes up her mind about something, she means it."

"Dylan will never live with you?"

He laughed. "Oh, I seriously doubt it."

"Marrying Cheryl is out of the question, of course."

"Of course. Brothers don't marry their sisters."

He watched her adorable mouth fall open as though

her jaw had come unhinged. He waited for a moment, then reached out and lifted her chin with his index finger until her mouth clicked shut. "You were jealous, weren't you?"

He guessed that as soon as she recovered from her shock, she would be furious. He was right. He braced himself for the storm brewing in her eyes.

"Jealous?" She shot out of her chair as though it had bitten her. "Hardly. I'm just finding it hard to believe that the big bad boy of Hollywood actually has a sister."

"A whole family in fact. My sister Cheryl, my brother-in-law Griff, their son Dylan, Mom and Dad. Cheryl and her family live in San Diego, but we don't get to see each other very often. I called her yesterday. She was delighted to find out I was this close, so she brought my nephew up to see me. Our visits are too few and far between. Dylan tends to forget me from one to the next."

"Your parents?"

He was glad to see that she had calmed down and seemed genuinely interested in his family. Only a very few close friends knew his background. He had no hesitancy in sharing it with Kirsten. Indeed, he wanted to.

"They live in a small town in Arizona, which has and shall remain nameless to protect its citizens from overzealous fans. The people there don't advertise it as my hometown because they think too much of my parents and want to protect their privacy. Dad is the high school principal; Mom taught freshman English until a couple of years ago when she took an early retirement."

Kirsten, having sat back down, now leaned over her desk, supporting her shaking head in her hand. "The high school principal. Freshman English. I can't believe it." Her head came up suddenly and she looked at him suspiciously. "You're not making this up, are you?"

He lifted the telephone receiver and extended it toward her. "Call them. Area code—"

"All right, I believe you," she said, irritably snatching the phone out of his hand and replacing it. "It's just that I never pictured you with parents. It's so—"

"Ordinary?"

"Yes. Not at all—"

"Sordid? Sleazy?"

Her shoulders slumped in an admission of guilt. "Why are we always willing to believe the worst about people?"

He dismissed her pertinent question with a smile. "Which story did you fall for? The one about my mother being a hooker on the Vegas strip? Frankly, I liked the one about the blind gypsy better."

Kirsten had the grace to laugh before asking him seriously, "You go along with those ridiculous stories in order to protect them, don't you?"

He nodded, thinking that her face, with the oversized glasses perched on her nose, was one he wouldn't mind seeing across his breakfast table for the rest of his life. He felt a kernel of emotion growing inside his chest until it was a solid pressure against his heart. Damned if it didn't feel like love was supposed to.

"Thank you for understanding that, Kirsten," he said huskily.

"Don't credit me with sensitivity. When I first saw Cheryl on the terrace, and you holding the boy, I—"

"You were jealous."

"So you said before," she said with annoyance. "I ignored the allegation then, but I categorically deny it now."

Like the Mafia heavy he'd once played, he grabbed a handful of her pullover and hauled her to her feet, practically dragging her across the desk to accommodate his hungry lips. He kissed her soundly, rubbing his mouth against hers until her lips parted. His tongue slipped inside and wasn't satisfied until it had thoroughly sampled her.

Her lips were rosy and wet when he finally released her to sink back into her chair.

Complacently he repeated, "You were jealous."

Six

Someone had done some housekeeping in his trailer. To that unknown being he was grateful. He'd left it looking like storm damage, but during his absence clothes had been picked up and laundered, the dishes in the tiny sink had been washed and put away, the wastebaskets had been emptied. All in all it was a cool, comparably quiet place to seek respite from the confusion and noise that constituted the location movie set.

The location wasn't too far from the Rumm house, actually. He'd driven it in an hour on his motorcycle. But it could have been on the other side of the world for all its desert remoteness. The landscape, which was supposed to be Abilene, Texas, was barren. Not a single tree provided shade from the glaring sun.

Rylan's trailer, parked on the perimeter of the set, was dim. The air conditioner hummed like a religious meditator. He had sought out the serene solitude while the director and technicians were setting up the scheduled scene.

"Come in," he called when someone knocked.

The director's assistant, a heavyset young woman named Pat, who figuratively, if not literally, took everyone on the crew to her large breasts and mothered them, came in.

"Are they ready for me?" he asked.

"Are you kidding?" Pat chortled. "It'll be a while yet. Need anything? Beer? Food? A girl?"

Such procurements had been handled discreetly before. Everyone in the business, including himself, took them in stride. Since when had the nonchalant system come to sound so shabby? Since Kirsten.

"No thanks."

"He," she said, referring to the director, "sent me in to ask you one more time to let your double do this scene. He's costumed and standing by, waiting for you to come to your senses."

"The script calls for close-ups. I need to do it."

"It's going to be tricky, Rylan."

"That's what they're paying me for."

Sighing in resignation, she asked, "Does this shirt need washing?"

"Please," he replied automatically.

Pat draped it over her shoulder. "How's everything going over at the Rumm residence?"

"Okay."

She frowned at him. "No elaboration?"

"No elaboration."

"The widow has been conspicuous by her absence," she remarked as she piled several of his garments in front of the door so she wouldn't forget them when she left. "Can I have a doughnut?" She took one from the open box without waiting for his permission and plopped down on the built-in sofa that faced the one he was lounging on.

"She says the book and movie are about Demon

Rumm, not her," Rylan said. He would have been surprised to know that he was frowning. The inverted v-shaped brows were pulled close together. "She wants as little to do with us as possible."

"Hmm."

He slid a knowing glance toward the director's assistant. "That's the most loaded 'hmm' I've ever heard. But if you think I'm going to appease your curiosity and discuss Mrs. Rumm with you, you're wrong."

Pat heaved herself to her feet, licking doughnut glaze off her fingers. "Unfortunately I know that. You never kiss and tell."

"Who says I've been kissing?"

It was her turn to give him a knowing look. Picking up the pile of laundry that would be driven into town and washed, she said, "Before I forget, let me have your script. Some changes have been made that need to be noted."

He sat up straighter. "What changes?"

"Relax, Shakespeare. You'll approve. The changes involve camera angles, not dialogue."

"They'll have to wait. I left my script at Kirsten's house. I knew I wouldn't need it today."

"We really should get the changes jotted down because they affect the blocking."

"Later," he said dismissively, and slouched back down. "Call me when they're ready."

"Sure you don't want your double to do this?"

He shook his head, his mind already elsewhere. Pat left the trailer unnoticed while Rylan was lost in thought about Kirsten's reaction to Cheryl's visit last week.

She'd been peeved and had unsuccessfully tried to hide it. Her jealousy had been as blatant to him as a fire truck with all sirens blaring and lights flashing.

And if she hadn't felt it so deeply, she would have laughed it off.

No, she wasn't indifferent to him. He had ruled out frigidity as the cause of her aversion. After Cheryl's visit, he had mentally scratched out the hypothesis that Kirsten liked men, but not particularly him. She worked hard at pretending she didn't, but the evidence was there, behind every glance she had directed at him over the past week. It had been behind that last tempestuous kiss over her desk. He had refrained from kissing, or even touching, her since.

His plan had been to let her stew for a while and reflect on what she was missing.

It had backfired. He was the one who was really suffering. He had no self-imposed restrictions to match hers. He wanted her. Badly. But he knew the value of perfect timing. And the right time for him to make his big move hadn't presented itself.

In the meantime he had slowly gone mad with desire. It had almost been a relief to leave her house this morning. The time spent away would give his brain and his body a much needed rest from the constant stress of wanting and not being able to have.

Now, while waiting for them to call him, he stretched out as far as the short sofa would allow and dozed as he daydreamed of Kirsten and how sweet it was going to be when she finally let him make love to her.

His ability to nap was almost obscene when he was about to be filmed sitting in a burning airplane.

In costume, Rylan wove through the trucks and trailers, the miles of cable, the milling crowd of people, all of whom seemed to be busy at getting absolutely nothing accomplished. Finally he reached the director, who was still in earnest discussion with the technician who had set the explosive charges beneath the mock-up airplane.

Gnawing on his trademark cigar, the director turned to Rylan and looked him over. "You're a goddamn fool for doing this," he growled. "That's why we've got stunt men on the payroll, you idiot."

"Which way to the airplane?" Rylan asked blandly.

He ignored the director's florid language and concentrated on the technician's explanation of how the explosions would be set off, how the one-take shot would be captured on film, and how he was to eject himself safely afterward. Timing was critical. The actor, the cameramen, the special effects technicians, all had to be synchronized and had to rely on each other's expertise.

"Okay?" the director roared. "Is everybody ready? Let's do it."

As it turned out, it was another full hour before they did it. During that hour, the director repeated Rylan's directions to him at least a dozen more times. The wardrobe mistress checked his flight suit to make certain it was "grimy" enough. The makeup man oiled and "sweated" him.

"I don't need that," Rylan said with star-status querulousness, pushing the squirt bottle out of his face. "It's hotter than hell out here."

"They're about to set your ass on fire, and you're complaining about a little sweat?"

Finally Rylan climbed into the cockpit of the fake jet and pulled on the helmet with DEMON printed in bold red letters across it. Camera angles were checked and rechecked in the video monitors mounted on

them. Everybody stood clear; the director gave the
signal to roll the cameras.

Rylan smiled and waved through the dusty canopy
of the airplane as the script called for. They were
recreating an airshow at which Rumm had success-
fully landed a malfunctioning plane, to the wild ap-
preciation of the crowd. Shots of that would be edited
in later. But even after landing, Rumm wasn't out of
the woods.

They had all warned him, but Rylan was surprised
by the impact of the first explosion. It rattled his
insides and, for a moment, gelled his brain. He didn't
even feel the second and third charges when they
went off.

Goda'mighty!

His eyes reflexively squeezed shut against the flash
of brilliant light. When he opened them again, he
was certain that something had gone wrong and
that he'd died and gone straight to hell. All he could
see in front of him was a solid wall of red-orange
flames, from which rose an equally impenetrable
curtain of black smoke.

The heat was so intense it seared his eyeballs and
melted his flesh. He was sure his skin was dripping
off his skull like the most hideous special effects in
horror movies.

Really dumb thing to be thinking about now, he
chided himself. *But what am I supposed to do?
What am I supposed to do? Oh, yeah. I'm supposed to open the canopy and get the hell out of
here before I fry.*

He groped for and found the release lever immediately. But, unlike the run-throughs they'd done, it
didn't respond to his touch. He pulled on it. Harder.
It didn't budge.

He fought down the sour panic that filled his throat

like vomit. God, it hurt to breathe. The air was so damn hot. He tried the lever again, his teeth clenching with the effort.

Jesus!

The director knew down to the split second when that canopy was supposed to fly off and Rylan was to climb out and roll clear of the burning aircraft. When it didn't happen, he exploded out of his chair, throwing his cigar on the ground. Screaming for fire extinguishers, he led the swarm of people that began running toward the burning aircraft.

Pat nearly choked on the undigested doughnut that rose into her throat. She screamed.

The wardrobe mistress was thinking that it was a damn shame she'd never slept with Rylan North, who was going to die in his prime, and therefore become a Hollywood legend that she would one day tell her grandchildren about.

The makeup man clutched the crucifix around his neck and, with this sudden reminder of mortality, regressed to his childhood fear of hell and damnation and begged God's forgiveness for the ménage à trois he'd been engaged in the night before.

And the petite, dark-haired woman, who was standing beside her Mercedes convertible, saw the reenactment of her worst nightmares.

She was witnessing the burning death of the man she loved.

Somehow Rylan spotted her. Later, he wondered about that. It was a miracle that he had picked her out of the scores of people who were all hysterically shouting instructions he couldn't hear above the roar of the fire and frantically making gestures he couldn't interpret.

Kirsten wasn't moving, only standing in the open door of her car, hugging to her chest something that inexplicably looked like a movie script. Tears, running copiously from beneath her sunglasses, had made her cheeks wet.

At first he thought she was only a figment of his imagination, that his life was flashing before his eyes as it was reputed to do moments before death. But he knew from the stark terror on her face that she was real.

"*Get her away from here!*" he shouted through the canopy. But of course no one could hear him. "God, no, don't do this to her," he prayed.

Impervious to the heat of the metal lever and the flames that were voraciously licking at his gloved hands, he pulled on the lever with superhuman strength. It gave way and the canopy popped off as easily as the top of a beer can.

Reacting on sheer reflex and the desperate need to get to Kirsten, he scrambled out of the burning aircraft and launched himself away from it, sailing several feet through the air in a daring escape that would make moviemaking history. He landed on his side and rolled to his feet as he'd been directed to do.

But Rylan wasn't thinking about directions. He was thinking only about the woman, the roiling black column of smoke behind him, and the living hell it represented to her.

He was immediately surrounded by people. Throngs of them. So many he couldn't fight his way through.

"Don't panic, Rylan!" someone shouted.

"The suit is asbestos. It's only smoking, not burning."

"Get to Kirsten," he yelled. "Kirsten. Help her. Let me—"

"He's not making any sense."

"He's hysterical, you jerk. Wouldn't you be?"

"Kirsten!"

He fought like a madman for them to release him, but they wrestled him to the ground. Kirsten was lost to his view.

"Get those damn gloves off. They're smoldering."

"Wrap his hands in something."

"No. Don't wrap them."

"Whatever you do, hurry, hurry, before he's scarred!"

He gazed down at his hands and with amazing detachment realized that smoke was rising out of his sleeves and that the flesh on the backs of his hands was abnormally red and puckered.

Someone nearly broke his neck yanking the helmet off his head. "Somebody go tell Kirsten—"

"Did anyone think to call a damn ambulance?" the director bellowed. "Damn imbeciles."

Rylan struggled to sit up. "Kirsten," he croaked, and ineffectually pointed his burned hand in her general direction.

"Lie down, Rylan." Pat applied a restraining hand to his shoulder, demonstrating more composure than anyone else. "You're going to be all right." She told the director, "There's an ambulance already here. Remember you ordered it just in case an accident like this happened."

"Then everybody get out of its damn way. I ought to sue you, you bastard," he yelled down at Rylan, "for taking a chance like that. Helluva job though," he added, chomping on a new cigar. "Helluva job. Everybody in the audience will be peeing in his pants."

"Here come the paramedics."

"Everybody stand back."

"Rylan, they'll take you to the hospital right away."

Someone pressed a cold cloth to his forehead. It was useless to fight them. And, God, he was tired.

Where was Kirsten?

Kirsten, Kirsten.

"You'll be glad to know there'll be no scars," Pat told him as she entered the private hospital room where he'd been treated. "The doctor says the burns were superficial, even though I know they hurt like hell. Keep that antibiotic salve on them for the next few days and take these pills for pain if you need them." She set a small container of medication on the bedside table. "They're harmless and will only produce a mellow state of well-being, or so I'm told by frequent users."

Rylan didn't even crack a smile.

Pat chatted on, undaunted by his moody silence, which she figured was a delayed reaction to the potentially fatal accident. "Our esteemed director called to tell you that this crash sequence and your escape from it is the most exhilarating piece of film he's seen in all his days in Hollywood. I think he considers your scorched hands of no more consequence than the sacrificial cigar he lost. The flowers are from him, by the way. The crew sent—"

"What was she doing there?"

Pat looked at him with perplexity. "What? Who? Who was where?"

"Kirsten Rumm. What was she doing on the set?" he asked darkly.

Pat lowered her bulk into the only available chair and looked warily at the man sitting on the edge of the hospital bed. The sullen mouth and hooded eyes weren't due to pain and delayed fear, she realized now. They were the offspring of controlled fury.

"Was she there?" she asked.

"Yes. I saw her from the cockpit."

"Maybe you just imagined—"

"I saw her!" he shouted. "What was she doing there?"

Pat quailed. "If she was, I guess it was my fault. I called her."

"Why?" His whisper was rife with menace.

"To . . . to . . . We really needed that script, Rylan. I asked if it was there at her house. She went to check your room and came back to say that yes it was."

"And you asked her to bring it to the set." Disregarding the tightness of the skin on the backs of his hands, he clenched them into fists.

"No, no, I didn't," Pat countered firmly. "I offered to send a messenger out there to pick it up, but she— Where are you going?"

"Home."

"Back to Los Angeles?"

He realized the slip he'd made, but didn't take time to ruminate on it now. There would be time enough to think later. After he'd seen Kirsten. "To her house. I can be reached there." He shed the hospital gown as he headed toward the narrow closet. Someone, probably maternal Pat, had had the foresight to bring him a change of clothes.

She pushed herself out of the chair. "But you can't leave the hospital!" she cried helplessly as she watched him dress. "The doctor ordered you to stay overnight for observation."

Rylan had a crude and anatomically impossible suggestion as to what she and the doctor could do with his order. He left the room and the hospital without breaking stride. Since his motorcycle was still at the set, he hired a taxi outside the hospital to drive him to La Jolla.

Even from the bottom of the hill, he could see that

Kirsten's house was dark. "Doesn't look like any-body's home, pal," the cabbie remarked over his shoulder. Rylan, wearing his opaque sunglasses, had gone unrecognized.

"She's here," he said with conviction. When they rounded the last curve in the winding driveway, he saw her Mercedes parked in front of the house. "Thanks." Whoever had provided the clothes and sunglasses had also stuffed some bills into his trouser pockets. He tossed a more than adequate amount of them into the front seat of the cab and got out.

The front door was locked. He went around to the back of the house and tried each sliding glass door until he found one that was unlocked. He braced himself for the burglar alarm to go off. When it didn't, he made his way through the darkened rooms.

He found her in her bedroom, lying across the wide bed, which made her look incredibly small by comparison. Her shoes were on the floor, toes point-ing toward the bed, as though she'd stepped out of them and had lain down in one movement. She was curled into a fetal ball, her knees drawn up, head bent so drastically that her chin almost touched her chest.

He said nothing, but went straight to the bed and sat down. Leaning over her, he stroked her hair. For a moment she only lay there unmoving. Then she rolled to her back and gazed up at him through the darkness.

His heart twisted with remorse when he saw that her eyes were swollen from crying. There were smudges of watered-down mascara beneath her lower lashes. Her lips looked bruised. He dipped his head and stroked them with his tongue, then kissed them softly. The most articulate actor in Hollywood couldn't come up with anything appropriate to say. He kept it simple and to the point. "I'm sorry you were put through that."

Her lower lip began to tremble. She slowly sat up and inclined toward him. His arms, his soul, were ready to receive her. He held her fragile frame against him and buried his face in her neck. She folded her arms across the back of his neck. Her sobs shook them both.

"Don't, don't," he murmured. "It looked a helluva lot worse than it was."

"It was ghastly. Awful. Just like my nightmares."

"I know, darling, I know." He smoothed his hands down her back. "I saw you. Through the fire. And I—"

It suddenly occurred to him that at that moment, when his death had seemed imminent, he had thought first of Kirsten and the anguish she was suffering. Wouldn't it have been natural for his first concern to be for himself? Yes, unless she had become more important to him than his own life. Yes, unless he loved her.

He turned his face into her neck and placed a fervent kiss on the softest, most fragrant of skin. The kiss was an unspoken profession of the love he couldn't declare. She wasn't ready to hear about it. But he knew it, and he celebrated it. He loved her! It was heaven; and it was hell. Because he didn't know whom she was crying over.

"I couldn't imagine what you were doing there," he said. "I thought I was seeing things."

Sniffling, she put space between them. "She . . . this lady named Pat . . . called and—"

"I know all about that now. There will be hell to pay."

"No, no, don't be angry with her. I volunteered to bring the script to the set."

"Why? I thought you wanted to stay away from it."

"Originally I did, but . . ."

Her voice trailed off and she looked away. He cupped her cheek and turned her face back toward him. "Why, Kirsten?"

Her answer was a long time in coming. "I've been so confused."

"About what?"

"About what was going on inside me, what I was feeling."

"Feeling?"

She lifted tear-laden eyes and looked straight into his. "Feeling for you."

Rylan's heart began thudding harder and faster than it had in the burning airplane that morning. "What's this feeling like?" he asked gruffly.

"I think you know."

"Give me a hint."

"When I'm around you, I can't think clearly. I always make a fool of myself."

"Never." His gaze greedily wandered over her face.

"I do," she said with desperation. "I had everything under control until you came along. Now I'm always flustered and unsure and I don't know why." She made an impatient gesture. "I can't explain how I feel."

He lifted her hand and pressed it over his heart, inside his shirt. "Is what you're feeling anything like this?" His rapid heartbeats drummed against her palm.

"Exactly like that," she whispered. Holding his gaze, she raised his hand and laid it over her left breast. "See?"

Making a low, growling sound, he bent his head and kissed her. She kissed him back, responding in kind to the urgent stroking of his tongue.

Still, there was a hesitancy underlying her kiss.
While he could think clearly, he pulled away. "What
is it, Kirsten? What's wrong?"

"You're too intuitive for your own good."

"It's just that when a woman kisses me, I want
her to be certain who she's kissing."

"You know," she gasped softly, surprised.

Solemnly he nodded.

She shuddered on the heavy breath she drew in.
"That's what I mean by being confused. We talk
about Charlie around the clock. When we're not talking about him, I'm writing about him. You move
like him. Your gestures are the same. You say his
words, which I've written down. You even use the
same inflections. But now, when I think of him, I
see your face, not his."

She looked up at him, profound confusion in her
expression. "I don't know if I'm falling in love with
him all over again or if it's you I'm attracted to."

Rylan rested his forehead against hers. For once
in his life, he wished he wasn't so good at his craft.
It wasn't unusual for him to take on the manner-
isms of the character he was playing for the dura-
tion of the filming. He literally became the person he
was portraying. He prided himself on that ability.
But this was one time he wanted to be seen only as
himself, stripped of any affectations and pretenses.

"If you had met me some other place," he began
slowly, "say I was the telephone repair man who had
come to install your phone, would you have been
attracted to me?"

She actually laughed. "I'm not dead, Rylan. I have
hormones. Is there a living, breathing woman who
wouldn't be attracted to the way you look?"

"That doesn't count," he grumbled. "Would you be
attracted to *me*, the man?"

"I don't know," she moaned, rolling her forehead from side to side against his, brushing noses. "I think so. The most honest answer I can give you is that I find you fascinating."

"I'll settle for fascinating."

She smiled at his quip. "You're not at all what I expected you to be. You're much more serious. Oh, you swagger. You appear not to give a damn about anything but yourself. But I realize now that you're not aloof to *people*, only to superficiality."

He liked what he was hearing. He laced his fingers together at the back of her neck and kissed her temple. "Tell me more."

"You have much more depth than I imagined you would. More caring. Your human side makes your audacity tolerable."

"Have I been audacious?"

She tilted her head to one side, allowing his lips better access to her neck. He pecked light kisses on it. "You know you have been. You kissed me the first night you were here."

"Who did you kiss back? Me? Or Rumm's memory?"

"Don't ask me that, Rylan. I'm not sure. Maybe I only responded because I hadn't been kissed in such a long time."

He sighed with dissatisfaction. "You were jealous before you found out that Cheryl was my sister. Admit it. It bothered you to think that Dylan was my baby, didn't it?"

She nodded. "Yes, I was jealous. Unreasonably so. That only confused me more. I had no right to be."

He settled his hands on her shoulders. "Kirsten, let me ask you a question." She met his penetrating gaze. "Today, when you saw that burning airplane, was it me inside there? Or Charlie Rumm? Were you terrified for me, or was your reaction left over from him?" He ran his thumbs over her tearstained cheekbones. "Who were you crying for?"

Her chest swelled with a deep breath. Gradually she released it. He felt it against his lips.

"You, Rylan. You."

Groaning deeply, he pulled her against him again and slanted his open mouth over hers. He sent his tongue spiraling down into the sweet silk of her mouth, and, as he did, pressed her back onto the pillows. Following her down, he partially covered her body with his.

They kissed endlessly. Her active participation, for once free from restraint, made him deliriously happy. Each time he started to withdraw, she initiated another kiss.

When finally their mouths separated so they could breathe, he pressed his face against her neck and sank his fingers into her hair. "Your hair's going to smell like this crap they put on my hands."

"I don't care," she whispered. "Do they hurt?"

"Not much."

"I called the hospital, and they told me you were all right. I wasn't sure if I could believe them."

"I'm fine. There's only one part of me that's hurting right now and I'm counting on you to make it well."

She laughed against his lips; it was the sexiest sound he'd ever heard. He groped for the buttons of her shirt. When they were undone, he snarled impatiently at the front fastener of her brassiere. Deftly he unhooked it and peeled it back to reveal her breasts. Her nipples were delicate and dusky pink. He covered one with his mouth while he lightly fanned his fingertips over the other.

"Rylan." Beneath him, Kirsten arched her back to push herself deeper into his mouth.

"You're so sweet."

He used his tongue to make quick, stabbing thrusts against her nipples, then sucked them gently. His hand moved beneath her skirt. The skin on the inside of her thighs was a realization of every adolescent fantasy he'd ever had. He followed that satiny path up to the cleft. The purring sound Kirsten made when he idly stroked her was all the encouragement he needed to work his fingers beneath the elastic leg of her panties.

He gave a hoarse cry when his fingers encountered the warm honey of her sex. He sent his fingers deep into her, knowing that he'd never get as deep as he wanted to be. He stroked her rhythmically and used her own slipperiness to heighten her pleasure in his caresses.

He was so full he strained against his clothing. To relieve the aching pressure, he unfastened his trousers and shoved down his underwear. "Touch me like you did before," he said hoarsely. He guided her hand down toward his rigid flesh. It was hard and warm with the love he so desperately wanted to express. He folded her fingers around himself. "Kirsten, Kirsten."

At first, when she rolled from beneath him, he thought she was going to undress. But when his cloudy eyes focused on her, she was huddled against the headboard, clutching her clothes together as though he were a raping vandal.

"I can't."

"Can't?" he wheezed.

She shook her head adamantly. "No."

No longer the compassionate friend and lover, Rylan reverted to the thwarted male. He realized he was making the chameleon transition, but his manhood was dictating this drastic mood swing, not his head and not his heart.

"What do you mean you can't?" he roared.

"Exactly what I said," she shouted back at him.

"Is it your period or something? Believe me, I'm not that fastidious." He took a perverse pleasure in her ruby blush.

"It's not that. I can't—*won't*—make love to you. Not now. Not ever."

His harsh breathing sounded like that of a domesticated beast about to turn back to its wild origins. "Damn you, then! It's no wonder your husband committed suicide."

Seven

One forgot until he sat and stared at it for hours on end just how vast the ocean was. Rylan had numerous hours that night to contemplate it. Sunrise finally crept up behind him and projected his silhouette on the sand. The shadow looked like an ill-formed hulk of a man, shoulders hunched forward, head sunk down between them, hair unruly. That shadow could have belonged to the sulky ogre in the most ferocious fable.

And that was exactly what he felt like.

Cursing himself, he lay down on the sand and stared up at the sky. It was rapidly losing its colorless, predawn pallor and taking on a pink glow, like a gravely ill patient who was showing visible signs of improvement. The stars that had held on for as long as possible winked a farewell and blinked out.

Rylan raised his hands and looked at them. He turned them this way and that. They hurt. The flesh was blistered and streaked with red. Maybe they were to blame. He'd been in pain, albeit subconsciously. His mother had always said he was the most ungracious patient. When he was sick, he was furious at the ailment for incapacitating him and had taken his anger out on everybody around him. No amount of tender loving care would appease his foul disposition. So blame last night's behavior and vituperation on his injured hands. Misery loved company. He had wanted to inflict pain on someone else.

Well, he had. In spades.

He bent one arm and laid it across his eyes. That didn't help to block out Kirsten's face, the way it had looked after he'd said those hurtful words. Pale and stunned, she'd stared at him. Her eyes had looked too large for her face. Her lips, which had been rosy and full from their kisses, seemed to fade and become narrow with despair even as he watched. Before his eyes, she was transformed. Her entire being seemed to shrink, to collapse from within.

The atmosphere had been static with tension, as sulfurous as in the seconds immediately following a striking lightning bolt. They had both been rendered motionless and, for a moment, speechless.

At last Kirsten had said huskily, "It wasn't a suicide. How could you say such a thing to me?"

Each word had risen a little higher in pitch and volume until the last ones had a hysterical ring to them. Perhaps if she hadn't been so vehemently contradictory, he might have withdrawn his accusation, apologized, and taken her in his arms again, not to woo, but to console.

But something about her stubbornness to protect Demon Rumm had beckoned the dark side of Rylan's nature. He had still been heavy with desire. That, too, had no doubt contributed to his meanness. For whatever reason, he'd flung back his head arrogantly and said, "That's the rumor, baby."

"Well, it's wrong." Kirsten slid off the bed and rounded on him. She hastily rebuttoned the front of her shirt and shoved down her wrinkled skirt. "It's wrong! Do you hear me? Charlie did *not* commit suicide. Why would he? He had everything to live for."

"Except a wife who liked to screw."

"How dare you—"

"Oh, I dare all right. I'd dare to say or do anything to a woman who would pull the stunt you just did."

She faced him with proud hauteur. "I didn't want to make love to you."

"Fine!"

"So what are you shouting about?"

"You waited a little too late to say no."

"I didn't mean for it to go so far."

He got off the bed and assumed his sardonic stance. "Didn't you? Is that why Rumm was so anxious to die? Did he work out his sexual frustration with aerobatics?"

She covered her ears. "Stop it! What happened between us just now has nothing to do with Charlie and me."

He summed up his opinion of that in one terse expletive and headed for the door. But before he stamped from the room, he stepped directly in front of her and zipped up his pants with insulting emphasis. "I'll save it for somebody who appreciates it."

At the time he had thought it was a great exit line. Now, after hours of dwelling on it, it didn't sound nearly as clever as he had originally believed.

I was horny, he justified to himself.

No excuse. An adult male learned to deal with unfulfilled arousal. That's what separated man from animals. Men didn't live in caves any longer and they learned to take a lady's "No" with dignity.

She shouldn't have let it go that far.

No, she shouldn't have. But the rational side of his brain argued that Kirsten hadn't planned on taking it to the brink and then calling it off. She had been ready and wanting just as much as he had. It wasn't her body that had said, "Uh-uh." Something other than whimsy had caused her to change her mind at the last minute. Something in her head. Or her heart.

It wasn't like that's all I wanted—slam-bam, thank you, ma'am. Not like that at all. I love her.

So maybe he should have exercised patience and understanding instead of storming out half cocked.

Appropriate analogy, North.

He sat up again and stared out over the undulating waves as they rolled ashore. Even their restlessness had a pattern to it. There was a source for every form of turbulence. So Rylan could partially excuse his wretched behavior last night. Mark it up to being in love. It was a bitchin' state to be in.

He'd read of men who had loved from afar, never consummating the eternal love they had for a woman. It was uplifting to think that some son of Adam had been that pure of spirit, that noble. But Rylan just didn't believe it was possible.

His sexuality was a vital part of him. Like his thumbprint or the shape of his eyebrows or the brown speckles in his eyes or his walk or his semihoarse voice. His sexuality wasn't something he could alter at will. He loved Kirsten Rumm with his entire being and that encompassed his sex glands.

"But, brother, does she ever have hang-ups where *that* is concerned."

What was wrong with her? Nothing physically. Her body did everything right. Maybe it all boiled down to this: She was still in love with Charles

Rumm. He'd been all-American handsome. He had had a dazzling smile and a magnetic personality. He had been rich and famous. No wonder Kirsten had been crazy in love with him.

But it was two years since his sui—his *death*. Kirsten was ready to love another man whether she knew it or not.

So Rylan's choices were clear. He could either throw in the towel and lament forever what might have been. Or he could stay, flay her alive if necessary to uncover the nucleus of her aversion to sex, and, once found, to heal it or die trying.

He stood up and dusted off the seat of his shorts. As he jogged up the steps that led to the terrace, he felt much the way he had when his agent once advised him, "I wouldn't even bother calling that producer, Rylan. The part in his picture is not for you. Even if he gave it to you, you'd be a flop. That role could ruin your career." He'd been determined to get the part and to make the movie a hit.

He had accomplished both.

Kirsten was sitting in the corner of the navy leather sofa in Rumm's study when Rylan, showered and changed, sat down close beside her.

Without preamble, not even a good morning, he said, "You should have slapped my face."

She looked at him, unsmiling. "I thought about it."

"Why don't you do it now?"

"Not my style."

"Go on. Lay one on me. It might make you feel better."

Smiling sadly, she shook her head. "I doubt it."

"Will you accept my apology?"

"For what?"

"For yelling at you like some street kid who's been shortchanged by a hooker."

Her smile widened. "I will if you'll accept my apology."

"For what?"

"For—for not going through with it."

"I forgive you," he said, then added softly, "I'm not sure I can forget."

She looked away. "Yes. That's the hard part, isn't it? Forgetting."

"I don't want to forget it, Kirsten. I want to re-member, to savor, how it feels to loveplay with you." He could tell he was making her uncomfortable by talking about it, so he changed his tack. "We'll swap apologies. Deal?"

"Deal."

They shook hands solemnly.

"What are you working on?" he asked. "And why in here?" He indicated the legal tablet resting in her lap, on which she'd made several notations.

"The last chapter of my book," she said. "I came in here because I thought a change of scenery might help."

"Oh? Problems?"

She sighed as though resigning herself to talk about something she'd rather not. "I've had writer's block where this chapter is concerned."

"You're too emotionally involved. You can't be objective."

"I guess so."

She looked small and helpless. Her eyes were ringed with violet shadows that intensified their blue color, but emphasized her wanness. Her mental and phys-ical fragility made him feel like a brute. More so because he was going to have to make her suffer again before they could start the healing process.

"What's snagging you?" he asked.

"I can't express how I felt after I heard about the accident," she confessed.

"The controversy that surrounded it couldn't have helped."

She had taken off her glasses to rub her eyes wearily. Now she looked up at him threateningly, her vulnerability having vanished in a matter of seconds. Before she could launch into an invective, he sandwiched her hands between his and said, "Kirsten, I want to get to the truth as much—maybe more—than you do."

"For the sake of the movie?"

"Yes, partly," he admitted. "But that's not the only reason. I think you know what the other is." Beneath his steady gaze her flare of temper fizzled. She looked down at their clasped hands. "What happened last night?" he asked gently.

"You were there. You know what happened."

"A beautiful, lovely and loving, sexy woman froze up. Why, Kirsten? And don't tell me that you didn't want me. I know better. No woman gets that wet for a man she doesn't want."

"Please, Rylan!" She moaned. Her head fell forward.

"Are you just incredibly shy? Did you have a strict upbringing? Were you taught that even talking about sex was taboo? Are you abnormally modest?"

"Of course not." He caught the smile behind her denial.

"Then what? Tell me. Did I do something that turned you off?"

"No."

He kissed her ear and left his lips there to whisper, "Did you like what I did?"

She nodded against his chest. "Everything."

As emotion swept through him, he squeezed his eyes shut. He gave himself a moment to tamp down a rising desire, then said, "Then why did you act as though I'd violated you? I've got the thickest skin imaginable. I can talk about anything without a single flinch. I promise not to be shocked no matter what you tell me." He tunneled all ten fingers through her hair and pulled her head up. "Tell me, Kirsten."

His eyes searched the troubled depths of hers as they filled with tears. "I can't, Rylan. Please don't ask me any more. Please. If you have any feelings for me at all, don't pressure me about this."

He felt like a cold, deadly dagger was digging into his gut. Protests filled his head. They clogged his throat in an attempt to be vocalized. But he watched one lone tear spill over her lower eyelid and trickle down her flawless cheek, and knew he would grant her any wish within his power to grant.

His lips sipped the tear from her cheek. "All right, Kirsten. I won't ask any more. But concede me two favors."

"What?"

"Tell me the truth about this." She waited, looking at him inquisitively. "Did you want me last night? Inside you? Loving you?"

Her gaze moved down to his mouth. "Do you really have to ask?"

He drew in a deep breath and held it. "So the reason you stopped it had nothing to do with us?"

"No, nothing." He kissed her, and though it was a tender kiss, it was compelling. "What's the second favor?" she asked huskily when he lifted his lips from hers.

"Recreate with me Demon Rumm's last twenty-four hours."

"*What?* Recreate his—"

"Because of these burns on my hands, I don't have to return to the set for several days. Talk me through his last day. Let's go through it hour by hour. I want to know the truth about what happened in that aircraft that morning."

"The truth is that Charlie had an accident. He did *not* commit suicide."

"All right. Then what is there to be afraid of?" He could see she was vacillating, so he pressed his point. "It will benefit both of us. You've come to a roadblock in your manuscript. Talking through those last twenty-four hours with me might help, might jostle something in your memory that will be useful to your book."

He stroked her lips with his thumbs. They were such soft, kissable lips, capable of receiving and giving pleasure. It broke all the rules of logic that she withheld both.

"Besides the professional considerations," he went on, "do this for us, Kirsten. We can't have each other until we exorcise Demon Rumm. And we *will* have each other."

He kissed her again, more firmly, using his tongue to convey the love he couldn't speak aloud and treating her mouth like the sacred, chosen vessel to receive it. When they pulled apart, his eyes silently repeated his request. She nodded in answer.

"Good, Sam's here. That's his truck." Kirsten pointed to a beat-up Blazer parked beside a corrugated tin airplane hangar.

Rylan wheeled her Mercedes beside Sam's derelict vehicle and said, "I'm going to have to buy me one of these."

"What? The Mercedes or that?" she asked, indicating the mud-splattered red-and-white truck.

He pretended to seriously weigh his decision. "What the hell? Maybe one of each."

Her laughter affected him almost as pleasurably as her kisses did. The sound of it made his middle feel warm. He looked forward to the day when this was behind them and they could laugh frequently and freely. He didn't doubt for a single second that it would happen. He'd knocked down far larger obstacles than Kirsten. Even larger obstacles than Demon Rumm.

They entered the cavernous building. Inside, it felt like an oven. Though it provided shade from the grueling sun, the airless heat was stifling. They walked between the disemboweled carcasses of airplanes and followed the sound of livid cursing until they spotted Sam. He was standing on a platform scaffold, bending over the exposed engine of an airplane.

"Sonofabitchin' bastard. Heap of—"

"There's a lady present," Rylan interrupted dryly.

Sam spun around so suddenly that he almost toppled off his perch. "You damned bastard, you scared the—"

"Careful, Sam," Rylan teased. "I've brought a lady to see you. Show her some respect."

The mechanic, wearing oil- and grease- and sweat-stained overalls, tromped down the metal steps of the scaffold. He wiped his hands on a faded red rag—obviously not for the first time. Stuffing it into the hip pocket of his coveralls, he eyed Kirsten up and down. "Not just any lady, North. The prettiest one around. If I weren't stinky, I'd give her a whoppin' hug."

"That never stopped you before," Kirsten said, holding open her arms.

Sam smothered her in a bear hug. The embrace produced tears in both their eyes and caused a flurry of awkwardness when they finally broke apart. Sam led them to a desk, which was as disorganized as the rest of the hangar. He pulled up an extra chair for Kirsten and nodded toward a wooden crate for Rylan. The mechanic could hardly take his eyes off Kirsten as she lowered herself onto the ripped, cotton-sprouting, plastic-covered seat of her chair.

"You could come to see me more often, you know," he said grouchily.

"I know. I apologize and promise to do better."

"You said that the last time. You live like a hermit up there in that fancy house on the hill. Oh, well, I'm old, ugly, and half blind. Can't say I blame you for not wanting to come see me. Not when you can toot around with studs like him." He rudely hitched his head in Rylan's direction. "What are you doing with him anyway?"

"The same thing you did with him, talking about Charlie."

Sam cast a jaundiced eye toward Rylan and pointed a finger with a week's collection of grease beneath the chipped fingernail at him. "You try anything funny with her and you'll be in a world of hurt. You Hollywood pretty boys don't scare me. I'll nail your balls to the floor."

Wincing, Rylan covered his heart with his hand. "My intentions regarding Mrs. Rumm are of the purest nature."

"My ass," Sam grumbled. "If you want action, I know where to find the flooziest, the nastiest, the raunchiest, the cheapest whores—whatever you want—in a hundred-mile radius. But you leave this lady alone."

"Sam," Kirsten intervened quickly, "do you have something to drink? Rylan insisted on taking the top off my car for the drive out here and I'm parched."

"Strawberry soda," Sam said, without even having to check the contents of the retirement age Frigidaire.

Kirsten and Rylan worked up a false enthusiasm for the bottles of syrupy-sweet red sodas he passed them.

"Guess you want to talk about Charlie," he said after taking a long pull on his own drink. He propped his feet on the corner of the ramshackle desk. The popular brand of his jogging shoes was the only thing that dated him. He could have been born in the airplane hangar and never cut the umbilical cord. He could have been the mechanic for Orville and Wilbur.

"That's right, Sam, we do."

Kirsten's gentle voice and the compassionate way she pressed the old man's wrinkled, oil-smudged hand made Rylan fall in love with her all over again.

"Well, shoot." Sam coughed to cover the emotion that congested his throat.

"We want you to tell us what happened that morning," Rylan said.

"What morning? You'll have to be specific."

"The morning he died," Kirsten said softly.

"What about it?" Sam reached forward to straighten the calendar on the wall, a ludicrous gesture since the topless blonde with the glittering G-string and glittering teeth was the most decent thing in the entire hangar.

"Was it a routine morning?" Rylan asked, knowing that getting anything out of Sam was going to be as joyful and easy as extracting an impacted wisdom tooth.

"Routine? Yeah, it was routine."

"What stunts was he going to practice?"

"I don't know. Nothing spectacular because he didn't have anybody flying along to spot him. He'd called and told the other fellows not to come in."

From the corner of his eye Rylan saw Kirsten's surprised reaction. She had told him that Rumm and his crew were virtually inseparable. It was significant that they hadn't been at the practice airfield the morning he died. "He called the others on the team from here?" he asked Sam.

"From that very phone." Sam pointed at the old-fashioned, black, rotary dial phone. "Told them to take the day off, said he wouldn't be needing them."

"Wasn't that unusual?"

Sam belched and shook his head. "He was the boss. He could do whatever he wanted to. Sometimes they all up and decided to take a vacation on the spur of the moment. Remember, Kirsten?"

She turned to Rylan. "He's right. The team kept no rigid hours. Charlie impulsively announced vacation time, things like that, when a big airshow wasn't coming up."

Rylan let them both collect their thoughts, but he didn't want Kirsten and Sam to become immersed in sentiment. This was a fact-finding mission, not a requiem. "How was the weather that day?"

"Perfect. Not a cloud in the sky." Sam sighed. "That was the hell of it. We'd flown through gale force winds, dodged lightning, penetrated fog so thick you couldn't see the nose of the airplane. Helluva thing, for Charlie to crash on a clear day."

Sam suddenly looked very old. The lines on his face seemed to be attached to strings that were pulling the skin down. His eyes looked rheumy, as tired and unsalvageable as the retinas that had grown old long before their time.

Kirsten reached out and covered his hand again. "I'm sorry to put you through this, Sam. Believe me, I wouldn't if it weren't vitally important."

Rylan's heart soared as high as the airplanes around him were capable of climbing. "Vitally important," she had said. So she must care, and care a great deal, about him. Then again, maybe she only wanted all rumors of suicide to be dispelled once and for all.

"He was flying a Pitts Special that day," Rylan said. "Did Rumm go through the preflight check himself?"

"Yep."

"Were you with him when he checked it out?"

"Nope. I was working in here. But he did it, because I could see him out yonder. We shouted several things back and forth. He didn't take any shortcuts."

"What kind of mood was he in?" Kirsten asked.

"Normal," Sam replied with a shrug.

"He didn't seem depressed about anything?"

"No." Kirsten glanced at Rylan, but before her expression became too smug, Sam added, "Kinda distracted."

"How?"

"Distracted?"

Both Rylan and Kirsten had pounced on the word like tigers on raw meat.

Rylan gave Kirsten the right of way. "Distracted how, Sam? It's very important that you remember any detail. Did anything out of the ordinary happen?"

Sam tipped his billcap forward to scratch the back of his head. "Thought it was odd at the time, but

. . ." He paused to shrug again. "After the accident and all, there was so much commotion, I guess I forgot about it."

Rylan didn't think Sam had ever forgotten a thing in his life. Until now the old man had withheld the forthcoming tidbit of information from the widow and from the world because he knew damn well that it was significant. Maybe Sam needed to be cleansed of Demon Rumm too. Maybe he had realized that it was time to let go. Facts, particularly unpleasant ones, had to be faced and reckoned with before they could be laid to rest.

"Tell me . . . us," Kirsten said.

"Well, you know that silly little superstition we had."

"The thumbs-up signal?" Sam nodded. Kirsten looked toward Rylan.

Rylan nodded too. "Just before takeoff," he said to Sam, "Rumm would look down at you from the cockpit and give you the thumbs-up sign. You saluted him."

"Yeah, right, well, that day he . . . uh, almost forgot to do it."

They all sat still and silent for a very long time. Finally Kirsten asked thinly, "Forgot? How could he forget? It was something the two of you did automatically."

"I know, that's why it bothered me. Later." Sam would look neither of them in the eye. Nervously he rubbed his rough hands up and down his thighs. "I was standing there on the tarmac looking up at him, expecting him to do it, but he was staring straight ahead, like he was thinking real hard about something, you know? I called up to him. He kinda shook his head, like he was coming out of a daydream, and then looked down at me. He smiled regular, white teeth and all. Then he gave me the signal and taxied off." Thick, salty, substantial tears rolled down the creased face. "That's the last I ever saw of him."

Rylan reached across the console of the car and covered Kirsten's knee with his hand. "You feel badly," he said intuitively. Despite her sunglasses he knew her eyes were still damp.

"Sam broke down and sobbed like a baby the first time I put him through that. I hated to do it again."

"I know." Rylan squeezed her knee.

"And it was so unnecessary."

"Why do you say that?"

"Because we don't know any more than we did about the cause of the accident. It was all there in the NTSB's report."

"But Sam confirmed that there were discrepancies that had no explanation."

"That's true in every airplane crash. Some things just can't be explained."

Rylan didn't want to contradict her to the point of being argumentative. She was cooperating with his quest for the truth and the reenactment of Rumm's last day. Anything jarring might send her retreating into her shell again, perhaps for good. What he was doing was not only beneficial to him, but therapeutic for her. Otherwise, he would have dropped it. It must be unbearably painful to learn that someone you loved had considered his life not worth living and chosen to end it.

"How do you explain the radio?" he asked. If he could get her to talk about it, she might reconcile herself to the truth that had become apparent to him. He didn't know the reason yet, but he was convinced that Demon Rumm had deliberately crashed his Pitts Special that day, or had done nothing to prevent the crash.

Kirsten rested her head on the back of the seat. "I can't explain why he lost contact with the tower."

"When they examined the radio after the crash, it was working perfectly."

"But the fuel line *was* blocked." There was an intensity behind her voice, as though she were trying to persuade herself.

Rylan kept his inflection as reasonable as possible. "But that was something he should have discovered during his preflight check."

"It might not have been blocked then."

"Maybe. But if the trouble started after he took off, he was expert enough to glide the plane to a safe landing, especially since the weather wasn't a factor. Those stunt planes are so light—"

"I know all about that, Rylan," she said sharply, turning her head away from him.

They drove for several miles before she looked forward again. Rylan took that as an indication that she was ready to reopen the subject.

"How do you explain his distraction that morning?"

"A bad mood," she said offhandedly.

"Kirsten, I've been studying the man for months. I've never heard of him having a bad mood. According to every source I've used from his high school yearbook to interviews with his crew, men who saw him every day, he was the least moody person to ever draw breath."

"He was human," she exclaimed. "Everybody has off days."

"And if Rumm ever had one, you would know about it, wouldn't you? You lived with him. Was he having an 'off day' that morning when he left?"

She was clasping her hands together so tightly that her fingers, at various points, were either very white or very red. "I don't know. He left the house before I woke up."

Rylan filed that away for later use. "It doesn't seem likely that he would forget to give Sam the thumbs-up signal when it was something they never failed to do."

"No, it doesn't."

"And Sam said that the day before the accident, Rumm had been perfectly normal. Smiling. Cracking jokes. Alert and brilliant in the cockpit. He left the airfield apparently without a care in the world."

Kirsten looked at him questioningly. Rylan drew a deep breath and said, "Which means that whatever distracted him that morning, whatever had him upset, happened here at home the night before."

Eight

They walked up to the front door. Rylan held it open for her. "What time did Rumm get home that day?"

"Early. Around three o'clock."

He checked his watch. "Close enough. What did the two of you do?"

"We watched old films. Or rather he did."

"Film clips of him?"

"Yes. Videos taped off 'Wide World of Sports' and such."

"Why do you say, 'Or rather he did'?"

"Because I was in and out of the study. I was cooking dinner that night."

"Why?"

Kirsten seemed reluctant to answer, but he held his stare until she did. "Alice wasn't here. She had taken those two days off."

Alice's toneless, tuneless humming had never seemed so loud as it did then, coming from the direction of the kitchen. "Go tell her she has the next two days off," Rylan said.

"I can't just walk in there and—"

"Then I'll do it for you." He headed for the kitchen. Kirsten lunged after him and caught a fistful of his shirt. "*I* will tell her."

Through the walls, Rylan overheard Alice's exclamation of surprise, then her series of feeble protests, before she finally capitulated by telling Kirsten that she'd been hoping for a free day to go see her daughter and grandchild.

"What did you cook that night?" Rylan asked Kirsten after Alice left. Having been in residence for so long, he no longer felt like a guest in the kitchen and made himself at home by pilfering an apple from the basket on the countertop.

"We ate shish kebabs."

"Lamb?" he asked unenthusiastically.

"Beef."

"Good. Got all the stuff?"

"This is pointless, Rylan. What good is this charade going to do?"

"Got all the stuff?" he repeated while extending toward her mouth, at the tip of a paring knife, a slice of apple.

She took the bite of apple between her teeth and mumbled around it, "I think so," in answer to his persistent question. She checked the contents of the refrigerator, freezer, and pantry to make sure she had the necessary groceries on hand. "If I thaw the meat in the microwave, I can start marinating it."

"Okay. I'll help you with the grill later."

"Charlie—" She broke off without finishing.

"Charlie . . . what?"

"He—he didn't help."

They looked at each other for a long moment. "I'll help," Rylan said quietly. "Are all the videotapes in his study?" She nodded. "I'll get started on those. I wanted to watch them anyway. Join me as soon as you can."

It was almost a half-hour later when she came into the room. Rylan had made the room as dark as possible by closing the shutters and turning off all the lights. He had put the videotapes in chronological order, according to the dates on the labeled boxes.

He explained this to her as she sat down on the opposite end of the leather sofa. "I'm only into the second tape," he said. On the wide screen TV set, a youthful Charlie Rumm was being interviewed at an airshow in Minnesota.

"I remember that show," Kirsten said animatedly. "Everyone but me considered it a warm, spring day. I was freezing. Charlie sent one of his gofers into St. Paul and he came back with a fur coat for me."

"Wasn't impulsive gift giving one of Rumm's traits?"

"Yes. He was extremely generous." Her gaze remained on the screen. "Charlie performed right before the Blue Angels. We went out to dinner with them that night. They all thanked him for warming up the crowd."

"In the figurative sense, you mean?"

"In the figurative sense," she said, laughing.

He loved the way she laughed because it was so unexpectedly husky and sexy. One would guess that her laugh would be like the gay, tinkling sound of a small bell. Instead it was whiskey-mellow.

She was still wearing the casual, wide-legged cotton shorts and blousy shirt she had worn to the airfield. As Rylan watched, she kicked off her huaraches and tucked her feet beneath her hips in a pose that he affectionately recognized as her favorite. Her legs had the satiny sheen of a woman who shaved every time she got in the bathtub.

Her shirt was unbuttoned all the way. Beneath it

she was wearing an elasticized tube top. Her breasts were squeezed into beguiling crescents over the top of it.

"Kirsten?"

"Hmm?"

"Did you sit that far away from Rumm while you watched old home movies?" She didn't answer him, just stared back at him with eyes that made him forget any other woman he'd ever met. "Come here."

The gruff invitation could have tempted a nun to forsake her vows of chastity. He was slouching on his spine with his neck hooked over the back of the sofa. His long legs were stretched out in front of him, ankles crossed. The scuffed leather Docksiders lay beside his bare feet like debris from a shipwreck. The denim of his jeans, bleached almost completely white, clung to his thighs and molded around his sex. No one, unless he was well acquainted with the fashion industry, would have guessed that his shirt, made of imported Indian cotton, had cost several hundred dollars. That faded, rumpled chic didn't come cheap. A single strand of dark hair, negligently falling across one of those sleek eyebrows, contributed to the sullen expression that had sold more popcorn and Jujy Fruits than any other screen star past or present.

Kirsten scooted along the cool surface of the leather sofa until she was close to him. He draped one arm around her shoulders and drew her even closer. "I love saying your name out loud," he whispered.

It pleased him when she tilted her head to one side to accommodate his lips, which were paying homage to the shape of her ear. "You say it correctly," she said breathlessly. "You have from the beginning."

"Oh?"

"Uh-huh. Most people pronounce it 'Cursten' instead of 'Keersten.' "

"Kirsten, Kirsten."

He tipped her head back against his bicep and lowered his mouth to hers. His kiss was gentle at first, as soft as the name he breathed against her lips. But after his first taste of her, his lips parted wider. Hers responded. Their tongues touched, flirted, mated. One of his hands slid down the column of her throat, lightly encircling it with strong, tanned fingers.

"Should we be doing this?" she asked during a gasping pause between kisses.

"Oh, yes."

"I'm not so sure."

"You know what your problem is?"

"I have several."

"You're too intense." He pecked her mouth lightly. "You don't play enough."

"How about a set of tennis?"

"How about some heavy petting?"

The light, teasing kisses melded into another deep, searching one. He glided his fingertips across her soft flesh, following the dipping and rising contour of the upper curves of her breasts.

He murmured love words, his voice throbbing, as he moved his hand down to cover one precious mound. He massaged it gently through her top.

"Rylan?"

"Hmm?"

"Stop."

"Uh-uh." He drew strong, passionate kisses from her mouth. "After a while all home movies, no matter how exciting, get repetitious and boring."

"But . . . ahh . . ." Her voice dwindled to ragged sighs when he lightly pinched the raised center of her breast. Her head lolled against his arm and her neck arched.

"You like that, don't you?" She made a sound that he took for a yes. "They get so hard. So, so sweet."

He dipped his head and closed his lips around one of the buds that was trying to poke its way through the stretchy cloth. He raked it with his teeth until Kirsten was writhing.

He pressed her to lie back on the sofa, following her down. He moved one of her legs aside and, reaching behind his back, set her foot on his hip. Then he nestled his body between her thighs and rubbed his hardness against the feminine notch.

Rylan was lost in her. His body knew only one goal, to bury itself into the snug fist of her femininity and let it milk him dry. He ravished her mouth with kisses, then burrowed his head in the hollow of her shoulder and drove himself higher and harder against her.

"Rylan, Rylan."

Her panting chant finally registered with his clamoring brain. He raised his head and looked down at her. His eyes were glazed with passion, so it took a moment for her features to merge and form her face.

"Not here. Not now." Her skin was rosy with desire, but her eyes were pleading.

Chagrined over his loss of control, Rylan levered himself up and assisted her into a sitting position. He flung his head back onto the sofa cushions and closed his eyes, breathing like a bellows until his pulse slowed down. Without lifting his head, he turned to look at her.

"I get it," he said, boyishly ashamed and apologetic. "It didn't happen here."

With her sitting close beside him, he'd almost forgotten the purpose of the afternoon. They were supposed to recreate what had happened between Kirsten and her late husband, not initiate anything of their own. Drawing in a deep breath, he ran his finger along her hairline beneath the shaggy bangs.

"Then he must not have touched you at all. He couldn't have stopped. You smell too damn good. I'm drunk on the way you smell."

He leaned over and kissed her neck. Her floral perfume blended with the scent of her skin, intoxicating him again. Lifting his head to meet her drowsy gaze, he kissed the backs of her fingers, sponging them with his tongue. "To hell with this fool plan," he said thickly. "Let's not stop."

He carried her hand down below his waist and laid it, open, over his bulging fly. "I want you so bad," he whispered. Covering her hand with his own, he made several stroking motions over the back of it.

"I want you, too," she said yearningly. "But this reenactment was your idea." She pulled her hand away, but not before squeezing him gently.

He almost soared off the couch and was actually amazed when he realized he hadn't. Laughing self-derisively, he growled, "Keep your distance, will ya?" His scowl was threatening, but it made her laugh.

They kept a safe margin between them for the remainder of the time they stayed in the study watching the videotapes. He did, however, hold her hand. It was impossible not to touch her. He asked questions about the tapes and she offered frequent comments of her own.

When they had exhausted the supply, he switched off the VCR and asked her, "Now what?"

She stood up and worked her feet into her shoes. "Dinner. I'll call you when it's ready."

He looped his arm around her shoulders as they

made their way through the house. "I offered to help, remember?"

He lit the grill out on the terrace while she made a salad of fresh spinach and put the rice on to boil. When he came in, he impaled the marinated meat cubes and vegetables on the skewers.

"Could I interest you in a wine cooler?" he asked when his chore was done. Kirsten was frying bacon for the warm honey-mustard dressing she planned to pour over the salad.

"That sounds good. Lots of ice, please."

She licked bacon grease from her fingertips. Rylan caught her in the act. "Need any help there?"

She smiled a siren's smile. "I can manage," she said in a seductively low voice, "but I appreciate the offer."

To keep himself from attacking her and gobbling her up, he opened the refrigerator and took out the wine cooler. "What should I drink?" he asked.

"A beer. No more than two. That was Charlie's limit."

"So his stand against drinking too much was sincere?"

"He was sincere about everything."

Kirsten had sprung to Rumm's defense so readily that Rylan extended the drink to her like a peace offering. "All right," he said softly. "I was just checking. There are a lot of closet alcoholics. Especially where I live."

"Well, Charlie wasn't one of them," she snapped. "Why are you always trying to uncover something ugly about him?"

Rylan stared down at the floor and counted to ten. The sexy, mellow mood of the afternoon had been destroyed. They were back to ground zero. He wanted to lash out at her that he knew damn well she was hiding some secret characteristic of Rumm's. That *something* was probably the reason he had killed himself. But saying that would be tantamount to calling her a liar. Her reaction would no doubt rival World War II. The thing he did *not* want to do was spoil their evening.

But damned if he was going to apologize. Avoiding that, he said, "Are these ready for the grill?" He picked up the lacquered tray that held the shish kebabs.

"Yes, but I cooked them that night. Charlie stayed in here and read the newspaper."

Rylan turned around at the glass door, holding it open. "Come out with me. I'd rather talk to you than read the newspaper."

When the kebabs were sizzling on the grill and they were seated in deck chairs sipping their drinks, he asked her, "Could there have been something in the newspaper that evening that upset him? Something like a bad write-up that would have distracted him the next morning?"

"I don't think so."

"What did you talk about that evening?"

"I don't remember."

"You must remember something," he insisted.

"I think that was the night I told him that I wanted to write a book."

"The biography of him?"

"No, that idea came later, after . . . after he died."

Rylan set his beer aside and turned the kebabs. "What kind of book did you want to write?"

"A novel."

"No kidding? Tell me about it."

She ducked her head self-consciously, but he could tell his interest pleased her. She outlined her story idea to him and blushed with pleasure when he told her that it had best-seller and hit movie stamped all over it.

"Provided I can play the male lead."

"You wouldn't have any fun with it. He's an embittered Vietnam vet."

"If I don't put my bid in now, Pacino will go after it. Who do you see as the leading lady?"

"Rylan," she exclaimed, "you're casting the movie and the book hasn't even been written yet."

He dismissed her pessimism with a shrug. "You'll get around to it. As soon as you finish *Demon Rumm*."

They didn't pick up the conversation again until they had filled their plates in the kitchen and carried them back to the terrace table to eat. Cutting into a piece of the succulent beef, Rylan asked, "Do you think Rumm felt threatened by your plans to write professionally?"

"I don't see how he could have. I never was exclusively a housewife. I'd always traveled with him and had some project or another to keep me occupied while he was with the crew."

"Which encompassed a considerable amount of time, I would imagine."

"He and the boys were together constantly. They—" Catching his alert stare, Kirsten laid her fork on her plate. "I resent what you're thinking."

"Which is?"

"That there was something going on between him and one of his crew."

"Was there?"

"Charlie wasn't gay. There was no relationship except friendship, *close* friendship, between him and any of the men who worked for him."

"I believe you."

She picked up her fork and resumed eating, but

he could tell she was annoyed. He redirected the conversation. "You say you traveled with him."

"Yes. Those last few years it slowed down some. He had earned his popularity by then and could be more selective about where he performed. We bought this house and settled down somewhat."

"Did you ever discuss having children?"

Rylan noted that her fork stopped midway between her plate and her mouth, and that when she completed taking the bite, her movements were halting, as though the fork met resistance in the air. "Yes."

"And?"

"We discussed it. That's all."

"Which one of you resisted the idea?"

"Neither of us." She set her fork down once again. "I said we discussed it. We didn't argue about it."

"You both favored the idea?"

"Yes."

"I don't see any children running around, Kirsten," he observed blandly.

"I never got pregnant."

"Was one of you sterile?"

"Not that I know of."

"You weren't medically checked out?" He was thinking that maybe an argument over children, or the lack thereof, could have precipitated Rumm's absentmindedness that morning, particularly if he had thought he might be to blame for Kirsten's barrenness.

"Don't jump to conclusions, Rylan. You sound like a soap opera. Charlie and I both wanted children. We—we just never got around to having them. Okay? Satisfied?"

He leaned back in his chair and studied her for a moment. "I fathered a child." The unexpected statement stunned her. Her eyes rounded with astonishment and her lips parted with the breath she sucked in sharply.

"Where is it?"

"Its mother killed it."

The wrath he had first felt when the young actress told him about the abortion thundered through him again. Unconsciously he clenched his hands into fists. That was the day he had learned that everybody was capable of violence. He'd wanted to kill the selfish bitch with his bare hands. The urge he had felt to destroy her frightened him even now. He thanked heaven that somehow he had kept himself from murdering her for aborting his child.

He blinked away his rage, and discovered that one of Kirsten's hands was resting sympathetically on his forearm. He covered it with his and stroked his thumb across the smooth skin.

"An abortion?" she asked.

He curtly bobbed his head, detesting the word. "I realize that some terminations of pregnancy are necessary. I'd even go so far as to say feasible. But, dammit, not when it was *my* baby!"

"Who was the mother?"

He looked at her, loving the concern he read on her face. "She doesn't matter. She never did." He squeezed his eyes shut in a moment of anguish. "But my child did. The thought of my baby being denied life still makes me sick."

"Was having a child that important to you?"

"If there hadn't been one, no," he confessed. "But when she told me about the baby, I wanted it very much. I guess because my own family is such a close one. What about you?" he asked suddenly. "Where are your parents?"

"My father divorced my mother when I was very small. I don't remember him. He remarried and had another family. I don't hear from him or see him. My mother died several months after I married Charlie." She smiled gently. "She adored him, and he was fond of her. I'm glad they had a chance to know each other."

For a long moment they were silent, each buried in his own thoughts as they gazed at the splendor of the sunset. Tall thunderheads on the horizon looked like purple blooms against a field of crimson and gold.

"Boy," Rylan said, blowing out his breath, "we certainly sank into a maudlin mood, didn't we?" He stood up and stacked their plates together. "Come on, let's get this cleaned up."

When the kitchen was in order, they migrated back to the terrace. The evening was particularly lovely. Kirsten turned on the underwater lights in the pool. Besides a moon, which was almost full, that was the only light they had.

"What did you do after dinner that night?" Rylan asked her.

"We swam."

"Really? I was just about to suggest the same thing." He linked his hands behind her waist and drew her close. Kissing her softly first, he whispered, "Thank you for not lecturing me about a woman's right to choose, et cetera, when I told you about the abortion."

"I regret the loss for you."

"I've never told a single soul about that."

"I'm glad you felt you could share it with me."

"You are?"

"Yes. And this is as far as it goes."

"I never doubted that." He kissed her again, using his tongue to part her receptive lips. It penetrated the wet, silky heat beyond them. "Ready?" he asked huskily.

She pulled back quickly. He laughed. "I meant, are you ready to *swim*?"

"Oh." There was a lovely, telltale color in her cheeks and a sparkle in her eyes, which were as deep an indigo as the darkening sky. "Yes . . . no . . . It'll only take me a minute to slip into a suit."

He tightened his hold when she would have walked out of his embrace. "You could do without. I do."

"I know. I've seen."

Smirking, he angled his head back. "Oh, yeah? You were watching that first day?"

"I didn't have much choice," she replied tartly.

"What did you think?"

"I thought you were quite a peacock to be strutting around buck naked like that." She wiggled free and stalked toward the bungalow where she kept a selection of swimsuits and towels. His laughter followed her.

Without a smidgen of modesty, Rylan stripped to the skin and dove into the water. His state of undress couldn't be concealed with the swimming pool lights on, so he was doubly pleased when Kirsten, knowing that he was naked, left the bungalow wearing a jade green bikini, walked straight to the diving board, and executed a graceful dive into the pool.

He swam to the shallow end and reclined on the steps, propping his elbows behind him. She swam several laps before joining him, winded. She turned onto her back too.

When she regained her breath and wiped the water from her face, she glanced over at him. "You aren't at all self-conscious, are you?"

"Nope. In college I modeled for the advanced art classes."

"Did your parents approve?"

His grin was unrepentantly mischievous. "We're close, but I don't tell them everything I do." He rolled to his side and splayed his hand wide over her bare middle. "What an erotic picture."

They stared down through the light-reflecting water at his hand, a shade darker than her skin, pressing against her stomach.

"Kirsten?"

"Hmm?"

"Did you make love with Rumm that night?"

Her hesitation was so slight, he might have imagined it. Staring directly into the dark pupils of his eyes, she nodded.

"Make love with me."

She made a whimpering sound of surrender a heartbeat before she clasped his head between her hands and drew his face up for her kiss. He half rolled, half floated to position himself above her, bracing himself on stiff arms.

The gently lapping current in the pool caused his body to drift against hers. His body hair feathered over her smooth skin with every shimmering motion of the water. She locked her arms around his neck. Her legs floated apart. His moved between them. Their skin, cooled by the water, only made their mouths seem hotter as their tongues probed deeply, ravenously. The very tip of his aroused sex brushed her middle, drifted away, returned.

"No wonder the ocean is so heavily populated," she murmured against his lips.

"How's that?"

She sighed. "This is bliss."

Lavishly swearing, he kissed her with diminishing control. "Damn," he cursed, tearing their mouths free. "This is no good. You're going to scrape your back on the edge of the step and I can't hold you or we'll both drown."

That should have been funny. They should have laughed. But they were too involved in the next kiss. His tongue was wildly flicking over her lips.

"The sauna," she suggested breathlessly.

"Good idea." He pushed himself off the step and extended a hand down to her. There was no way he could hide his arousal from her. He didn't try, but pulled her along behind him as he padded toward the enclosure that housed the sauna, slinging water across the terrace with each step.

"Wait," she said, tugging on his hand. "Go on in. I'll—I'll follow. Give me thirty seconds," she pleaded when she saw that he was about to object.

He let go of her hand and entered the redwood cubicle. The heat was fierce. Ironically, he glanced down at his body. There was no way he could feel cool. He was on fire. Sexually he was burning hotter than he'd ever burned before.

He picked up the water hose and sprayed the rocks. They hissed. A cloud of steam billowed up to fill the room. And out of it, Kirsten materialized wearing only a towel. If his eyes looked anything like hers, he knew their coupling was going to be passionate and insatiable. Her eyes were so deeply blue they appeared black in the dim sauna, where a single bulb burned weakly, casting a red glow over everything.

The swirling steam seemed to adore her. It wreathed her head and formed tendrils around her shoulders and legs like seaweed clinging to a cherished sea goddess.

Her breasts were rising and falling rapidly above where the end of the towel was tucked in. Suddenly shy, she sat down on the second level of the sauna, her knees primly pressed together and her hands chastely folded in her lap. She might have been a parochial schoolgirl awaiting an appointment with the mother superior.

Rylan smiled and shook the sweat out of his eyes. He walked toward her and sat down on the level below hers. "Is this how you came into the sauna that night?" Her eyes reflected the red of the light bulb, but he preferred to think that that glow was from the flames of desire he'd ignited.

"No."

"Well?"

It seemed to take forever for her hands to work free the knot in the damp terry cloth. When it was undone, she still held the towel against her for a moment that seemed like an eternity in hell for Rylan.

Then she let it go. The towel fell to the bench and pooled around her hips. She sat before him naked. Her breasts were high and round with pert nipples that, despite the heat, were partially erect. The gentle flare of her hips emphasized the narrowness of her waist. Cradled in her lap was a nest of dark, silky curls, glistening wetly. Her skin shone with a patina of sweat and melted body lotion. Her wet cap of hair, forming points around her face, made her appear very young, almost too young to touch.

Almost.

Rylan, his own body dripping perspiration, knelt on the bench in front of her. It placed him just a little below eye level with her. He inclined his lips up to hers. Hers descended to touch his. She kissed him with endearing bashfulness. He patiently kissed her hesitation away. When his tongue slid between her lips, she raised her hands to his shoulders. He felt her body relax but, conversely, felt the sexual tension mounting. It seemed that sparks of desire arced between them.

He settled his hands on both sides of her waist. As their kiss intensified, his hands shifted up and down her rib cage, until he conformed his thumbs to fit the undercurves of her breasts.

"You're beautiful." He leaned back to watch as his thumbs circled her nipples, then gently fanned them to hardness. She incoherently murmured something. "Feel good?"

Eyes closed, breathing rapidly through her mouth, she nodded. "Yes, yes. But—"

"What, love?"

"Kiss them."

His ears were ringing with the pounding of his blood. He was only too glad to do as she asked. Lowering his head, he took one rosy bead into his mouth and sucked it. She pressed his temples between her hands and bent her head over his.

"Harder," she groaned. "I want to feel it all over."

His arms wrapped around her. He kneaded the supple muscles of her back as his mouth greedily tugged on her breast. But he never wanted to hurt her. When he got the merest indication he'd become too ardent and was causing her discomfort, he used his tongue to soothe her.

He licked the sweat from beneath her breasts. With the tip of his tongue he followed a drop on its trickling trek from her collarbone to her navel. He crested her nipple with his tongue as the bead of sweat did, and continued to trace its downward course until he sipped it up with his lips.

She was sobbing dryly, and he feared he was going too fast. He drew her into his arms for another reassuring kiss, but her lips, which twisted beneath his, and her hands, which moved over him restlessly, let him know that she was as aroused as he and that her moaning sounds were of frustration and not fear.

"Your body is beautiful, Rylan," she said when their kiss ended.

"Surely it holds no surprises for you. I've done nude scenes. At least from the back."

"On the screen, you're just a beautiful object. But this is different. This is personal."

Her gaze moved over him lovingly. He'd always considered his well-shaped body an asset to his profession, but he'd never taken such pride in it as he did now. When she laid her hands on his chest and combed her fingers through the wet, curly hair, his heart surged because she liked him.

Their bodies were impossibly slippery, but that only intensified the deliciousness of holding each other when they kissed. His nipples grazed hers, eliciting sighs from them both. It took but a slight nudging of his hips to separate her thighs. He inched between them and didn't stop until he felt her warm, damp femininity against his belly.

He kissed his way down her middle, nibbling with his lips, tickling with his tongue. Her neck, breasts, stomach, belly were all paid tribute by his mouth. He pressed his face into her lap and kissed the fleecy mound. He nipped the inside of her thighs with his teeth and pressed a special kiss on the faint birthmark.

"I love you, Kirsten."

Then he touched her with his open mouth. He kissed her with love and with delight. His tongue tasted her sweat and her sweetness and kept taking samples from deep inside her until the steamy chamber was filled with her gasping cries of pleasure.

Nine

He held her close to him until the aftershocks sub-sided. She kept her head down, nestling it in the hollow of his shoulder. Sensitive to her embarrass-ment, he said nothing, but lifted her into his arms and carried her out of the sauna.

He walked to the pool and down the steps. He didn't stop until the water was up to Kirsten's chin. He withdrew his right arm from beneath her knees. Her legs floated down, but he knew she couldn't touch bottom, so he held her against him.

Eventually she raised her head and looked up at him. He cupped a handful of water and emptied it over the top of her head. She laughed as it rivered down over her. Rylan was filled with such love that he could barely speak.

"Taste how sweet you are," he said gruffly.

He kissed her, pressing his tongue deep into her mouth. Holding her tight, he submerged them. The water closed over their heads, washing away the heat of the sauna and their perspiration. They didn't

break the kiss. When they surfaced, their mouths
were still locked together.

They drew apart slowly. Rylan waded back toward
the shallow end of the pool, holding her up until she
could touch bottom. Hands linked, they left the pool
and by tacit agreement entered the house. In her
bedroom, he switched on a bedside lamp. The subtle
light limned their nakedness with gold. He scattered
the dozen or so decorative pillows on her bed in that
many directions and whipped off the bedspread, then
guided her down to join him in the Victorian brass
bed.

"Are you all right?" he asked, once they were lying
face to face.

"Shaken and weak."

"Me too."

"It was unfairly one-sided, wasn't it? I mean, you
didn't . . ."

"What do you think we should do about that?"
She scooted closer to him, rubbing her body against
his. His sex felt the dewy caress of her womanhood.
"Kirsten," he rasped, "say it."

"Come inside me, Rylan."

He covered her and with one swift thrust imbedded
himself inside her. "God, you're small," he moaned.
"And tight." He was both delighted and concerned.
"Am I hurting you?"

Her eyes fluttered open. She laid her hands on his
cheeks and raised her head high enough off the
pillow to softly kiss his mouth. "No. No."

At first his movements were tentative. But he responded to the rising up of her hips to meet his, to
her flushing breasts beneath his lips, to her hands
which fondled his head, his back, his buttocks. Soon
nothing else in the world existed or mattered, not
his career, not her haunting past, not their uncer-

tain future. Now *this* was all that counted, and he wanted to make his loving the most glorious experience of her life.

Driven as he was to climax quickly, he disciplined himself to meet her needs. But the crisis rushed upon them like a runaway train. Neither was braced for the physical and emotional impact that slammed into them simultaneously.

When it was over, he couldn't bring himself to leave her, but stayed snuggled within the giving folds of her body. "Am I too heavy?" he asked. Slumberously she shook her head. He laughed softly. "Should I be offended or flattered that my lovemaking has put you to sleep?"

Her eyes opened lazily. "I'm not sleeping." The words were sexily slurred. "I'm just relishing the feel of you. It's wonderful."

He was filled with a ferocious possessiveness. He buried his face in the curve of her neck and languished in her afterplay. She fiddled with his ears. Idly she strummed his back, trailing her fingernails up and down the groove of his spine from shoulders to his buttocks. She palmed the firm muscles there and laughed throatily when he flexed them. Her body, too, was caressing him from within, quick little contractions that robbed him of rational thought, of breath.

"Kirsten?"

"Hmm?"

"I'm, uh . . ."

"Yes, I know. It feels so good."

"You don't mind?"

She shook her head.

This time it was a slow, sliding, undulating loving that sent him deep into her again and again. Pure animal pleasure rippled through them with each smooth stroke. Even the climax was long and languid. They drifted to sleep afterward.

Feathery kisses awakened him. No heavier than a butterfly in flight, they grazed his lips, then were gone. Lord, he thought. And was she . . . ? Yes, her fingers were drifting across his belly, not quite touching his manhood, but flirting with the idea.

"Little girls can get in a lot of trouble doing that to little boys," he growled, keeping his eyes closed.

"That's what I'm counting on."

Her mouth settled over his. He kissed her carnally and wetly before opening his eyes to see her gamine grin. "Have a nice nap?" she asked. He grunted in response. "Hungry? I am."

She rolled to the edge of the bed. He reached for her. "Come back here, you."

She giggled. "I will."

He watched her leave, thinking she had the most delectable fanny he'd ever seen, surprisingly voluptuous for a woman so slender. Grinning like the proverbial 'possum, he lay on his back, his hands beneath his head, stretching in sybaritic delight and thinking how grand life could be.

The decor of her bedroom was a surprise. In contrast to the stark modernity of the rest of the house, this room was lavishly romantic with a few antique furnishings. She might have a chic haircut and dress smartly, but within Kirsten's breast beat the heart of an ultrafeminine lady.

Rylan adored every quaint aspect of her personality.

In several minutes she returned. He was glad to see that she was still wearing nothing but the smile of a complacent, sexually sated woman.

"Do you like Oreo cookie ice cream?" she asked.

"Was Spencer Tracy my favorite actor?"

They battled over the carton of ice cream, fencing with their spoons like swords, until the bottom had been scraped clean. Rylan set the empty carton on the nightstand and, sitting Indian fashion in the center of the bed, drew Kirsten into the circle of his legs. He positioned her to face him and draped her thighs over his. He linked his hands at the small of her back.

At first their lips and tongues were cold because of the ice cream. But one deliciously sweet kiss melded into another until their mouths were hot, seeking, and addicted to the taste of the other.

Gasping for breath, Kirsten flung her head back and gave his searching lips access to her neck. As he nibbled his way down her throat, he caressed her breasts.

"Your hands are never still," she whispered.

"You don't like it?"

"I love it."

He kept his head down, unwilling to break the chain of kisses he was planting along her collarbone. "A holdover from my childhood. Cheryl would never let me play with her dolls." His fingertips dusted the tips of her breasts. Her back arched reflexively. She leaned away from him, thrusting her chest out invitingly.

He was ecstatic with the passionate nature he had discovered beneath her secretive veneer. When the cloak of doubt and suspicion was off, she was a different woman. Fascinating. Fun. Sexy. She responded to and initiated almost more loveplay than he could keep up with.

He lowered his head and kissed each of her taut nipples in turn, then pressed his face into the shallow valley between her breasts. "I love you, Kirsten."

She ensnared his hair in her fingers and lifted his head. "You said that before, Rylan. But it wasn't necessary for you to say it to get me into bed with you. And it's not necessary to say it now."

"Is that why you think I said it?"

"Isn't it?"

"You seem to do the thinking for both of us. You're the lady with all the answers. You tell me."

She lowered her gaze to his chest. As she collected her thoughts, she absently toyed with his chest hair, twining clumps of it around her fingertips. "I know how the system works. The men in the crew took advantage of girls they met on the road, promising undying love in exchange for a few days of sex."

"Easy lays with stars in their eyes."

"Exactly. I'm smarter than the average groupie, so I'm not naive enough to believe that you've fallen in love with me."

"Why do you find that so hard to believe?"

"Because you're a star!" she exclaimed. "Wasn't it *McCall's* that dubbed you the sexiest man in the world last year? You could have any woman you wanted."

"Thanks for the compliment," he said dryly. "But if that's true, why didn't I go hunting down another woman after your first rejection?"

"I wounded your ego. You had to prove to me, and to yourself, that you could seduce me."

"At first maybe," he admitted with chagrin. "Your indifference intrigued me." He pulled on the fringe of hair in front of her ears and replaced each mussed strand just so, concentrating on the task while he selected and discarded the words he would say to her. "I've been living here with you for over three weeks. Do you still think I'm that shallow? Don't you know me any better now than you did that morning we met in your attorney's office?"

He looked at her earnestly, clasping both of her hands between his. "I don't blame you for your preconceived evaluation of me. I cultivate my 'bastard' image. I capitalize on it. I also use it to protect myself. It affords me some privacy. But that's an image; it's not *me*, Kirsten. Don't you know that by now?"

It was her lips that were trembling, but she raised her hand to his, pressing her fingers against them. "I've been so bitchy to you. How can you love me?"

He turned his head and playfully bit the fleshy part of her arm. "We've only got the rest of our lives. I'm not certain I can show you all the ways I can love you in that scarce amount of time."

She smiled at his joke, but she was shaking her head. "We don't have the rest of our lives, Rylan. We only have tonight."

He stared at her in disbelief. "You expect me to walk out of your life and leave you as though this never happened?" He yanked her body forward. "Never, Kirsten. Never in a million years would I give you up now."

"What are you proposing?"

"That we live happily ever after."

"You're forgetting something."

"What?"

"That I want anonymity."

He *had* forgotten that. They had hurdled over all the other obstacles in their path, but there was still that one. And it was mighty. "We'll work it out."

"Impossible."

"Don't ever tell me something is impossible," he warned her in a gravelly voice. "I'll be just that much more determined to prove you wrong."

Sighing, she leaned forward until her forehead bumped his. "Rylan, please, don't expect more than I can give."

"If tonight is a sampling of what you can give, I'll take all of it I can get."

"I'm serious. What do you expect of me?"

"I expect you to love me in return." He tilted his head and kissed her. "Don't you? Just a little?"

"I don't know," she answered miserably.

"You love me," he said confidently. "Otherwise, why would you be here, doing this, making love with me?"

"Because you're beautiful." He felt her breath filtering through the hair on his chest. Her fingers traced its growth pattern all the way down to his navel. "Because I wanted to. And needed to."

Sliding his hands beneath her hips, he lifted her over his rigid manhood. Sighing in pleasure, she sank upon him, letting her head fall to his shoulder as she rocked her body slowly forward and backward over him.

"Rylan," she sobbed. "Oh, Lord, I needed you. Needed this."

There was desperation behind her soft cries, and he knew he had yet to unlock her cache of secrets. But for the moment, he responded to her physical needs. Wedging his hand between their bodies, he caressed her where they were joined. With a delicate touch, he stroked the most elusive and most vulnerable part of her. Waves of passion originated in that tiny bud of femininity and vibrated through her. When her body quickened and began to rhythmically squeeze his, he gave free rein to his own passions and filled her with the scalding evidence of his love.

* * *

He came awake slowly, at first unable to discern what had awakened him. He reached for Kirsten; she wasn't lying against him as she had been when they'd finally exhausted themselves with lovemaking and fallen asleep.

He opened his eyes. Kirsten was still in the bed with him, but was lying out of arms' reach. And she was crying. It had been the shudders of her weeping that had awakened him. She was shaking, but not uttering a single sound.

He stretched his arm across the bed, but he still couldn't reach her. She lay just beyond his grasp. "Kirsten?"

The sobbing ceased abruptly. She sniffled, but she didn't turn around. Her shoulders were hunched, her back slightly bowed. He could have delineated each individual vertebra.

"What's wrong?" His voice was as quiet and still as the room. He got no answer. Instinctively he knew not to touch her, though he ached to. "After last night, how can you wake up crying?" He was genuinely perplexed. His body was sore. He was bone tired. His eyes were gritty from lack of sleep.

He'd never felt better in his life.

It was beyond his comprehension that she could be weeping. She wasn't crying for joy. It wasn't a case of her not being able to contain her happiness and pouring it out in the form of tears. Her lonely, silent weeping didn't have a single joyful aspect. It was the heartrending, gut-wrenching kind.

Moving fractionally closer, not wanting to spook her, he ran his finger through the shaggy hair at her neck. As he had expected her to, she reacted quickly by springing into a sitting position on the edge of the bed.

She turned her head and looked at him over her shoulder through teary eyes. "That's not the way it happened."

It took him a moment to decipher her meaning. When he did, his heart sank like a lead ball in his chest. "With Rumm, you mean?"

She nodded. "We were supposed to be recreating our last night together, weren't we? Well, that's not the way it happened."

So what the hell was that supposed to mean? Rylan thought as he watched her get up and slip into the bathroom without saying another word or giving him so much as a backward glance.

Had that night two years ago been better? Worse? Happier? Sadder? Sexier?

Impossible. Nothing had ever been sexier. Was she comparing Rumm to him? Comparing them as lovers? Comparing the way she felt for each of them? *What*, for godsake?

Dammit, the woman was going to drive him nuts!

He was angry and felt he had every damn right to be. Who did she think she was, to toss out an oblique statement like that—while he'd been lying there, a goosey smile on his face, his toes still curled with pleasure—and then disappear into the bathroom without an explanation? He had put up with a helluva lot of crap from her, but she'd gone one step too far this time. He damn sure wasn't going to let it pass.

He lunged off the bed and stormed across the room, cursing vividly when a corner of the sheet, which was twisted around his calf, refused to let go despite his kicking efforts.

At the bathroom door he stared down at his white-knuckled grip on the doorknob. He could hear the water running in the shower. If he barged in there without his pants on, ranting and raving like a maniac, he'd look like a damn fool, especially if she was composed enough to be taking a shower.

In less than sixty seconds, he was standing beneath the shower in the guest bathroom. It didn't take him long to dress. Even so, she beat him to the kitchen. She was swathed from her chin to her ankles in a white terry-cloth robe and couldn't have been more covered up unless the robe had had a hood. Her hair was adorably wet and spiky around her face, which was colorless except for her eyes. She was barefoot, but the look she shot him as he stamped in was anything but vulnerable.

His temper was simmering, his nerves were frayed, and he was gutsick in love with a woman whose heart remained a mystery even though he knew her body intimately. So, he said the first hurtful thing that sprang to his mind. "You refused your husband, right? On the night before he died, you refused to have sex with Rumm. Is that it?"

"*No.*"

"Sure it is," he said, advancing on her menacingly, backing her into the corner. "You pulled one of your famous freeze-up acts and wouldn't let him touch you. That really screws up a man's head, ya know? So the next morning Rumm takes off in an airplane and decides to kill himself because of you."

"*No!*"

"How many times had you done it to him before?"

"Stop it!"

She planted her hands firmly over her ears, but he worked them off and held her wrists within the iron grip of his fingers. "Last night you gave me what you withheld from poor ol' Charlie. Was that your

way of making recompense? Is your conscience clear
now?"

"I had nothing to feel guilty about," she shouted.

"You made your husband a sexual beggar, denying him what was his right."

"I did not!"

"No?"

"No. It was Charlie, not me, who—"

She sucked in her breath and jerked her hands
free, then whirled around. He caught her by the
shoulder and spun her back to face him. "What did
you say?" he asked incredulously.

Her face was extraordinarily pale. She gazed back
at him fearfully. "Nothing."

"It was Rumm who *what*, Kirsten?"

She moistened her trembling lips. "It was Charlie
who . . . who didn't make love."

He stared down at her, hearing only the thudding
of his own heart. He watched heavy, luminous tears
slide from her eyes and roll down her cheeks.

"You mean he . . ."

"He couldn't."

Rylan felt he'd been dealt a stunning blow to the
head. Once he'd played a boxer. His sparring partner, a boxing coach, had gotten a little overzealous
to make the final fight look real for the cameras.
He'd made solid contact with Rylan's jaw and for the
next thirty minutes Rylan had seen stars and heard
bells. That's how he felt now. Like the planet had
just been yanked out from under him and he was
adrift in a black void.

Kirsten stepped around him and shakily poured
herself a cup of coffee. He lowered himself to one of
the kitchen stools. "Ever?" he croaked.

"No," she said coolly, matter-of-factly. "When we
first got married, everything was wonderful. We en-

joyed a healthy, active sex life. That only made things more difficult later." Using both shaking hands, she raised the coffee cup to her lips and sipped from it.

She looked so helpless and small in that encompassing robe. He wanted to hold her, but knew she wouldn't welcome his pity, so he remained where he was while she glided over to the glass wall and stared out at the rolling surf.

"What happened to him, Kirsten? An accident?"

Heaven knew there had been plenty of opportunities for Demon Rumm to have been irreparably injured, Rylan thought. His accidents were recorded on the videotapes they had watched yesterday. Numerous times he'd been hospitalized with broken bones, lacerations, burns. His body must have been scarred. But apparently only his wife knew about the most damaging scar.

"His problem wasn't physical," Kirsten said, instantly negating Rylan's theory. "At least I don't think it was. He—he never would go see a doctor about it."

"For godsake why?"

She rounded on him. "Would *you*?" Rylan's hastily downcast eyes provided her with an answer. "That's right. He was a celebrity. A sex symbol. A superstud. Men like him aren't supposed to have that sort of problem. He defined virility. One hint that he didn't live up to his image and his career would have been over. Kaput. So much for Demon Rumm."

The affliction wasn't all that uncommon, Rylan knew, even among men who banked on their virility. But Kirsten was right. What man would admit to such a thing, even to a supposedly confidential doctor? To do so would be risking not only his pride, but his livelihood.

"So he just let you suffer."

"We both suffered," she said quietly. "His . . . incapacity increased in proportion to his growing popularity. I think he felt pressure to live up to his macho image. It would have been impossible to be all he was supposed to be, so he felt defeated before he even tried." She twined the belt of her robe through her fingers, her expression sad. "Of course I'm only guessing. As I said, he never would consent to see a counselor. At all costs he wanted to keep anybody from knowing."

"But look what he was doing to you all that time."

"It was far worse on him than it was on me."

"I seriously doubt that."

She pressed her fingers against her forehead as though recalling arguments and turbulent scenes from a marriage in terrible crisis. "I couldn't do anything to help him. He resented my help. Any encouragement I gave him he took as sympathy. Taking the sexual initiative upon myself only made him feel more inadequate and made me feel like a whore. So I learned not to acknowledge the problem at all. We conveniently ignored it."

Rylan slid off the stool and moved toward her slowly. "Until that night before his crash." His gut instinct told him he was right. Her shiver confirmed it.

"Yes. Until that night."

She had sunk into her well of memory. She stared outside sightlessly and seemed unaware that he was standing beside her. "What really happened that night, Kirsten?"

"Alice had taken two days off. Charlie and I had enjoyed watching the old videos together that afternoon. I had cooked a good dinner. I thought that maybe, since he was relaxed and had been in an affectionate, cheerful mood all day . . ." Her voice dwindled off.

"Did you swim after eating dinner?"

"Yes, I suggested that we swim. I remember thinking how gorgeous he was with the fading sunlight reflecting off his hair. He was showing off, acting silly, falling off the diving board to make me laugh." She pressed both fists into her middle and squeezed her eyes shut. "I wanted him. I wanted to love him, to have him love me."

Rylan's heart went out to her, but he didn't ply her with any more questions. He let her tell the story at her own pace.

"When we came out of the pool, I lured him into the sauna. I urged him to take off his swim trunks and he relented. I initiated everything because he never even wanted to try. You see, it was humiliating for him to try and not be able to."

She bowed her head and held her hand over her mouth. She was swallowing hard, trying to clear her throat of emotional congestion. When she picked up the story, her voice was steadier.

"I was so sure that night that I could heal him. I knew that if it happened once, he would be over the psychological block forever. So I kept on kissing him, even when he turned away. At first he was playful, saying things like, 'Cut it out, Kirsten,' and 'What was in your wine?' But then I started caressing him. He was beautiful to touch." She exhaled raggedly. "But instead of getting aroused, he got angry. He shouted at me. Told me to leave him alone. And stormed out of the sauna.

"Later, after I'd returned to the house, he came into the bedroom and apologized. He even hugged me, kissed me, and lay down beside me. That night we slept with our arms around each other. I remember loving him more then than at any other time. I intended to tell him so the next morning. But when I woke up, he was gone."

Rylan thought she had forgotten he was there. But she hadn't. At the conclusion of her dreadful story, she looked up at him with inexpressible despair.

"There you have it, the ugly truth. Isn't that what you wanted?"

Yes, that was what he had wanted. But now that he had it, he wished he'd left that final stone unturned. Instead of ridding her memory of its poison, the lancing of her wound had only poisoned her against him. For once, his relentless probing had backfired.

Oh, now he knew the motivation behind Rumm's death wish. Now he knew why the pilot had been fearless and willing to take death-defying chances. Demon Rumm hadn't really cared if he lived or died. Death was preferable to impotence and living a lie. The hero behind the dazzling smile had been a sham. Demon Rumm had personified the great American male, but he couldn't make love to his own wife.

Yes, indeedy, it had all the makings of a terrific character study movie.

But at what cost to Rylan?

The woman he loved.

"How will you end your book, Kirsten?"

She laughed mirthlessly. "What difference will it make? The movie will tell the true story. You have the justification for Demon Rumm's suicide. That's what you really came here looking for, wasn't it?"

He stared down at her for a long moment before turning on his heel and walking out.

* * *

It was four weeks later when he rang the doorbell of her house. Alice answered the door. She greeted him warmly, but her smile was uncertain.

"Is Kirsten here?"

It was a rhetorical question since her car was parked in the driveway. Apparently Alice saw the futility of lying. "She is, but she's asked not to be disturbed."

"Please, Alice."

Looking into his compelling hazel eyes, the house-keeper weighed her decision. The scale tipped in his favor. She stepped aside. "In her study."

He walked into the room, immediately recognizing Kirsten's endearing vacant stare out the window. She was lost in thought and didn't immediately notice him. Her head came around slowly, then she did a double take. He was gratified to see a flash of gladness in her eyes before she hastily screened them with animosity.

"What are you doing here?"

"Have you seen a pair of jeans lying around? Faded out, holes in the knees, seat wearing thin? I can't find them anywhere. Did I by chance leave them here?"

"No. I think you took everything with you."

"Not everything, Kirsten," he said, dropping his bantering inflection. "I left a vital part of me behind." He moved toward her desk and tossed down his movie script. "We finished shooting yesterday. Had a helluva wrap party last night. I was the only one who stayed sober and slept singly. Anyway," he said with exaggerated casualness, "I thought you might want to read the last scene of the script."

He flopped down on the sofa and laid his head

back, closing his eyes and folding his hands across his stomach as though settling down for a Sunday afternoon snooze.

It required all his acting skills to play this scene. He wanted to cover that adored face with kisses, to rub the lavender shadows from beneath her eyes and inquire if her obvious sleeplessness had anything to do with him being away from her.

The last month had been pure hell for him and, consequently, for everybody who came in contact with him. If he'd been a reputed terror on the set before, he'd outdone himself lately. He'd even reduced loving and lovable Pat to tears before she threatened to turn him over her knee and give him the paddling he well deserved. He and the director had more than once threatened each other with everything from castration to litigation.

He had demanded perfection from himself and from everybody else associated with the movie. And because he was deeply in love with a woman who couldn't stand the sight of him, it had made for an exhausting, emotionally taxing time.

But now that the movie was in the can and he'd gained permission to be consulted on the editing, he could devote himself to winning the reluctant widow.

Through slitted eyelids he watched her poke the script as though it might be a carnivorous animal that was playing dead until she let down her guard. Finally she turned it right side up and riffled through the pages to the ending. Rylan watched her eyes behind her glasses, moving back and forth as she read the script. Even from across the room, he saw them grow glossy with unshed tears. When she glanced up at him, he remained perfectly still and pretended that he hadn't seen the soft, loving look she sent his way.

Teeth clamping her lower lip, hand resting against her heart, she read the last page.

Demon Rumm walks across the tarmac, his back to the camera. He and the airplane are silhouetted against the rising sun. Just before climbing into the cockpit, he pulls on his helmet. Sam walks into the scene, his back to the camera. He watches Rumm settle into the cockpit and fasten his harness. Rumm starts the engine. CU of Sam. *He registers puzzlement.* CU of Rumm. *He is staring straight ahead. Sam calls his name. Rumm turns his head, looks down. A slow smile breaks across his face. He raises his hand and gives Sam the thumbs-up sign. Freeze frame. The end. Roll credits.*

Slowly Kirsten closed the script. She smoothed her hand across its cover as though it were something precious.

She looked across the room at Rylan, her expression one of bewilderment and . . . hope? He lost the battle of wills with himself. "Come here, Kirsten," he said in his rugged, raspy voice.

She walked over to him and folded a knee beneath her as she sat down beside him on the couch.

"After hours of arguing," he said, "I convinced the screenplay writer, the director, the producer, and everybody else involved to go for poignancy instead of some big, dramatic finish. No one really knows what was going through Rumm's mind that morning when he climbed into the cockpit. Not even you, my darling."

"You didn't . . ."

"No, I didn't. Did you really think I would reveal your secret to the world?"

"I wasn't sure."

He laid a hand on her thigh, squeezed it. "Why would I hurt you that way?"

"Because of your career. Your integrity. Your unbroken rule not to compromise on characterization."

"I would never hurt you for the sake of a damn movie. I love you more than any role, than fame, fortune, or anything else."

"Rylan." Lowering her head, she spoke to her clenched hands. "I was so defensive, so nasty to you, because you're too clever. I wanted you so badly. Every time you touched me I went off like a flare."

"I didn't know if that was arousal or revulsion."

"It was fear. I was afraid you'd guess the truth, that you would somehow guess how deprived I'd been. The more involved we became, the more I feared you would discover the truth. And I had to protect Charlie. That was only fair, wasn't it?"

He touched her cheek lovingly. "I admire you for your loyalty. It makes me jealous that you loved him that much. You could have exploited his sexual incapacity, sensationalized it, and made a lot more money on your book."

"I don't know how to finish it."

"Want my advice?" She nodded. "Finish it to correlate with the movie's ending."

"But the public will want to know if it was a suicide or not."

"Why do you feel obliged to provide an answer you don't even have? Let them draw their own conclusions. The ending of the movie leaves it wide open to speculation. No one knows about his impotence except you and me. Even that doesn't diminish what he was or what he did or what he stood for. He lived up to everyone's expectations. The only person he hurt was you." He cupped her face between his hands.

"And as of now, I'm going to start healing you of that hurt."

"But—"

He stopped her protests with a single finger against her lips. "Save your breath. I'll only shoot down every argument. And I'm used to getting my way."

Her lips trembled beneath his soft kiss. "You really do love me, don't you?"

He smiled and said softly, "I really do."

She laid her head on his chest and, for both of them, drew a sigh of contentment. "You are the dearest man."

Epilogue

"Hi, Mom. Did you get checked into the hotel all right? . . . Good. How'd you like the premiere? . . . Did you see me wink at you? I wish you and Dad could have sat with Kirsten and me, but just knowing you were there meant a lot . . . I'm glad you enjoyed the story . . . Yes, it was supposed to make you cry."

He cupped his hand over the mouthpiece of the telephone. "Mom said she cried," Rylan informed his wife.

Speaking into the phone again, he said, "Did I tell you that *Demon Rumm* is on *The New York Times* best-seller list? . . . I did? Well, I'm proud of it."

He blew a kiss across the room when Kirsten turned and smiled at him over her shoulder.

"She's already hard at work on her third book. I think she's got two chapters roughed out. I get jealous of that typewriter . . . No, I offered to buy her a word processor, but she's turned the idea down flat . . . I'm not sure. Something about fondling the pages of her manuscript." He covered the mouthpiece again and said to his wife, "Sounds kinky to me. If you're looking for something to fondle—

"What'd you say, Mom? Kirsten, uh, distracted me . . . Oh, yes, I know that a baby wouldn't interfere with her career as a writer. We're working on that . . . Yes, she is tiny, but the doctor checked her out and said that she could carry a child. He gave her a checkup and a tune-up. I figure she's good for at least forty thousand miles." Laughing, he dodged the pillow that came sailing toward his head.

"Tell Dad I noticed that too." He cupped his hand over the receiver again. "Dad said to tell you that you looked sensational tonight, even though he could barely see you through the crowd." Speaking into the telephone again, he said, "Tell Dad she says thank you . . . No, she hasn't gotten over her aversion to living in the public eye, but I told her that if she didn't want people gawking at her, she shouldn't be so damn good to look at . . . Oh, sorry, Mom. You're absolutely right, I shouldn't swear . . . Right. Say, listen, are you still coming to Malibu for brunch in the morning? . . . Great, we can't wait for you to see the house. It's similar to the one Kirsten owned in La Jolla, open and airy and looks out over the ocean. But extremely private. We both love it . . . What? Okay, I'll tell her . . . Around eleven? . . . Terrific. We send our love. Good night."

He hung up the telephone in their master suite. "Mom and Dad said thanks for the flowers and fruit basket. Remind me to send a tip to the bell captain at the Beverly Hills Hotel."

"I took care of it for you, darling."

"I knew I kept you around for something."

Sending him a smoldering glance, Kirsten slowly and provocatively wet her lips with her tongue. "And it isn't to tip bellmen."

The day she became able to tease about sexual matters, he knew she was completely healed of her past unhappiness. Now, after more than a year of marriage, she was openly affectionate and loving, never afraid to express her desire for him at the risk of being rebuffed. Responding to her blatant come-on now, he reached for her, but she playfully dodged him.

"Are Cheryl and Griff coming tomorrow, too?" she asked.

"Yeah," he answered, laughing as he peeled off his tuxedo coat. He slung it negligently over a chair. "And Mom said to put anything you don't want broken under lock and key. Dylan is into climbing and destroying."

"Did I hear a reference to a baby in your conversation?" Kirsten met his eyes in the mirror as she took the diamond studs out of her ears. "Specifically *our* baby?"

"The folks are getting antsy for another grandchild. I'm afraid Mom's hints aren't very subtle." He slid his arms around her from behind and splayed them over her tummy. "Any symptoms?"

"Nine days late and counting."

He kissed her neck. "Hmm, good. But any later and we'd have never packed you into this dress."

It was a tube of midnight-blue sequins. The high collar fastened around her neck halter-style, leaving her arms and back bare. The glittering dress sheathed her petite figure like a second skin from her neck to the vamp of her silver sandals.

Drawing her back against his body and placing his lips directly over her ear, he whispered, "Did I mention how fantastic you looked tonight?"

"A few dozen times," she said, smiling at him coyly.

He turned her around to face him. "And did I tell you how much I appreciate your suffering through that circus with me?"

She untied his bowtie. "*Demon Rumm* is going to be a very important movie for you. Rumors of an Oscar nomination for best actor are already in the wind. I still don't like being in the spotlight, but I'm willing to be if you're there with me."

Disposing of the satin tie, she slid her arms around his waist. "Appearing at the premiere wasn't as bad as I expected. I'm no longer pretending to be happy. I *am* happy. I'm not living a lie anymore. I love my husband. And I know he loves me. That makes smiling in public a cinch."

Their kiss was long and deep. He unsnapped her dress and let the skimpy bodice fall to her waist. "You lived up to your end of the bargain and attended the premiere with me." He gazed down at her breasts as he caressed them. "I guess I'll have to go out tomorrow and buy a new pair of jeans."

She removed the studs from his shirt and helped him shrug out of it. "But will you wear them?"

"Ah," he said, "*wearing* them wasn't part of the deal."

As they laughed together, she shimmied out of her dress and he stripped off the rest of his clothes. He carried her to their wide bed and laid her down. As he bent over her, she ran her fingers up through his hair. He would never tire of her touching him, never tire of the love she radiated as she smiled up at him.

"Having a wife who obviously adores you hasn't changed you much," she said chidingly. "You're still Hollywood's baddest boy. I heard what you said to that photographer who blocked our path."

"Unprintable, wasn't it?" His mouth moved over her breasts.

"Indubitably."

"I was only trying to protect you."

"The only protection I need is your love, Rylan." Though that wasn't his real first name, it was the one she had fallen in love with, so she continued to call him by it.

As frequently as they made love, their passion never waned. Lovemaking was a rite of renewal, a daily pledge that each was loved and cherished.

"You've got my love, Kirsten. Forever." He thrust into her with gentle fervency.

"Oh, my darling." She sighed with immense pleasure. "It never crosses my mind to doubt it."

THE EDITOR'S CORNER

Last month I briefly told you the good news that The Delaney Dynasty lives on! Next month you'll get a sneak preview of the second trio of Delaney books, **THE DELANEYS OF KILLAROO**, in a Free Sampler you'll see everywhere! It's part of a promotion that is unique in publishing history and is being done jointly by LOVESWEPT and Clairol®. In the late fall last year, a creative and effervescent young woman representing Clairol, Inc., came to see us at Bantam. Their market research had identified the "perfect user" of a new hair product they were developing as the same woman who reads LOVESWEPT romances! You, my friends out there, were described as intelligent, clever, fun loving, optimistic, romantic women who cared about and tried to make a contribution to family, friends, community, and country. Sounds right to me, I said. The new product from Clairol®—PAZAZZ® SHEER COLORWASH—is a continuation of the PAZAZZ® line of temporary (and, I must add, fun) coloring gels, mousses, and color wands. But what truly amazed me was that one of the colors they had "invented"—*Sheer Plum*—had just been "invented" by Fayrene Preston for her heroine Sydney in **THE DELANEYS OF KILLAROO**. Further, while Iris Johansen's and Kay Hooper's heroines weren't described in the precise terms of the new Clairol® colors, they were so close that one had to begin to believe that our two companies were fated to get together with **THE DELANEYS OF KILLAROO** and **PAZAZZ®** **SHEER COLORWASH**. So we decided to do a promotion featuring a Sampler of the new books about the Australian branch of the Delaney family, whose heroines had Sheer Colorwash hair colors. And in each Sampler Clairol® gives you a Beauty Bonus full of tips on hair beauty and styling using the new products. Next month at health and beauty aid sections of stores and at cosmetic counters you will find the Free Sampler. You'll also find the Free Samplers when you go to your local bookselling outlet. In all, more than three-quarters of a million copies of these Samplers will be given away during a six-week period. Then, when **THE DELANEYS OF KILLAROO** books are published in August, the first 200,000 copies of each title will carry a special money-saving coupon from Clairol® so that you—you "perfect users" you!—can try

(continued)

PAZAZZ® SHEER COLORWASH at a lower price. I hope you'll enjoy this promotion since you are its special focus. Lots of other women who may never have heard of LOVE-SWEPT romances will learn about them, too, as all of us learn for the first time about a brand-new way to put more PAZAZZ® into our lives with color highlights ranging from subtle to dramatic . . . from the glints of gold in Sheer Cinnamon or Amber to the glow of a fine wine in Sheer Plum or Burgundy. We on the LOVESWEPT staff have been treated by Clairol® to samples of all these products . . . and if you could see us now! We, in turn, treated the Clairol® ladies to the Delaney books and other LOVESWEPTs, and they loved them! We've had so much fun with this promotion, and we hope you, too, will enjoy this first-ever promotion with you in mind.

Now for a few words about the delightful LOVESWEPTs in store for you next month.

We are so pleased to introduce a wonderful new talent, Glenna McReynolds, making her debut as a published author with **SCOUT'S HONOR**, LOVESWEPT #198. In this charming love story Mitch Summers, a wonderfully masterful and yet vulnerable man, follows stunningly beautiful Anna Lange from San Francisco to the Bahamas to ask her a simple favor: would she turn her gambling skills on a cheating cardsharp and win back the land his brother lost in a crooked poker game? After a disastrous experience with a fortune hunter, Anna holds all men at arm's length, but she cannot resist Mitch's boyish charm . . . or his passionate kisses. With the glamour of high stakes poker and with the heart-warming emotion of sensuous romance, this is a fabulous first love story from Glenna McReynolds.

Prepare to be glued to your chair, unable to put down **ALLURE**, LOVESWEPT #199, by Fayrene Preston. Breath-takingly passionate and emotional, **ALLURE** is the love story of Rick O'Neill and Chandra Stuart, star-crossed lovers who meet once more after years apart. Only Rick can't remember very much about Chandra, and she has never been able to forget a single thing about him! Then, haunted by a scent that brings along with it a powerful memory, Rick begins to unravel the mystery of the past . . . and blaze a trail toward a future with the woman he loves. An enthralling, powerful romance.

(continued)

We are delighted to announce that Joan Bramsch—author of such wonderful, beloved LOVESWEPTs as **THE SOPHISTI-CATED MOUNTAIN GAL** and **THE STALLION MAN**—has the distinction of being the author of our two-hundredth LOVESWEPT, **WITH NO RESERVATIONS**! Hotel executive Ann Waverly is understandably intrigued by Jeffrey Madison. The first time she meets him he looks like something the cat dragged in; the second time, he's wearing only a sheet! Jeffrey is powerfully attracted to Ann, but his suspicious actions make her wary of him and the potent effect he has on her senses. Actually, both Ann and Jeffrey have their secrets, and you'll be kept on the edge of your seat as Joan skillfully weaves this tale of humor and deep love.

Linda Cajio gives us another lighthearted and touching romance with **RESCUING DIANA**, LOVESWEPT #201. At a reception Adam Roberts is captivated by Diana Windsor—nicknamed Princess Di—an endearingly innocent and shy creator of computer games. Diana is equally enchanted by Adam—he's her knight in shining armor come to life. But neither Adam nor Diana expected he would *really* have to rescue this princess from all sorts of modern-day dragons. As you follow Adam and Diana from one delightful escapade to another, you'll fall as much in love with them as they do with each other.

Enjoy!
Warm regards,

Carolyn Nichols

Carolyn Nichols
  Editor
LOVESWEPT
Bantam Books, Inc.
666 Fifth Avenue
New York, NY 10103

The first Delaney trilogy

Heirs to a great dynasty, the Delaney brothers were united by blood, united by devotion to their rugged land . . . and known far and wide as

THE SHAMROCK TRINITY

Bantam's bestselling LOVESWEPT romance line built its reputation on quality and innovation. Now, a remarkable and unique event in romance publishing comes from the same source: THE SHAMROCK TRINITY, three daringly original novels written by three of the most successful women's romance writers today. Kay Hooper, Iris Johansen, and Fayrene Preston have created a trio of books that are dynamite love stories bursting with strong, fascinating male and female characters, deeply sensual love scenes, the humor for which LOVESWEPT is famous, and a deliciously fresh approach to romance writing.

THE SHAMROCK TRINITY—Burke, York, and Rafe: Powerful men . . . rakes and charmers . . . they needed only love to make their lives complete.

☐ RAFE, THE MAVERICK by Kay Hooper

Rafe Delaney was a heartbreaker whose ebony eyes held laughing devils and whose lilting voice could charm any lady—or any horse—until a stallion named Diablo left him in the dust. It took Maggie O'Riley to work her magic on the impossible horse . . . and on his bold owner. Maggie's grace and strength made Rafe yearn to share the raw beauty of his land with her, to teach her the exquisite pleasure of yielding to the heat inside her. Maggie was stirred by Rafe's passion, but would his reputation and her ambition keep their kindred spirits apart?   (21846 • $2.75)

LOVESWEPT

☐ *YORK, THE RENEGADE by Iris Johansen*

Some men were made to fight dragons, Sierra Smith thought when she first met York Delaney. The rebel brother had roamed the world for years before calling the rough mining town of Hell's Bluff home. Now, the spirited young woman who'd penetrated this renegade's paradise had awakened a savage and tender possessiveness in York: something he never expected to find in himself. Sierra had known loneliness and isolation too—enough to realize that York's restlessness had only to do with finding a place to belong. Could she convince him that love was such a place, that the refuge he'd always sought was in her arms?

(21847 • $2.75)

☐ *BURKE, THE KINGPIN by Fayrene Preston*

Cara Winston appeared as a fantasy, racing on horseback to catch the day's last light—her silver hair glistening, her dress the color of the Arizona sunset . . . and Burke Delaney wanted her. She was on his horse, on his land: she would have to belong to him too. But Cara was quicksilver, impossible to hold, a wild creature whose scent was midnight flowers and sweet grass. Burke had always taken what he wanted, by willing it or fighting for it; Cara cherished her freedom and refused to believe his love would last. Could he make her see he'd captured her to have and hold forever?

(21848 • $2.75)